Reigning in Life as a King

John Osteen

ABOUT THE AUTHOR

John Osteen has served as pastor, evangelist, author, and teacher for over forty years. Ordained as a Southern Baptist, he received the Baptism in the Holy Ghost in 1958, an experience which changed the vision of his calling to a worldwide outreach for Jesus Christ. He has traveled extensively throughout the world, bringing the message of God's love, healing, and power to people of all nations. For him, The Great Commission has become not only a reality, but a way of life.

Today John Osteen pastors Houston's Lakewood International Outreach Church, one of the nation's largest churches. Lakewood Church is known as *"An Oasis of Love in a Troubled World"* by many, and people from all over the globe lovingly call it *"home"*.

John Osteen has a weekly television program that reaches millions of people across the nation. He also founded World Satellite Network as a means to unite Believers everywhere, to provide balanced teaching of the Word of God, and to share the outstanding five-fold ministries of our day.

John Osteen holds a Bachelor's Degree from John Brown University, a Master's Degree from Northern Baptist Seminary, a Doctor of Letters from Indiana Christian Univeristy, and a Doctor of Divinity from Oral Roberts University. He is the author of 26 books, and his cassette tapes are widely distributed throughout the Body of Christ. His mailing address is John Osteen Ministries, Box 23117, Houston, Texas, 77228.

BOOKS BY JOHN OSTEEN

The Confessions of a Baptist Preacher
Reigning in Life as a King
How to Claim the Benefits of the Will
How to Demonstrate Satan's Defeat
How to Flow in the Super Super Natural
How to Release the Power of God
Pulling Down Strongholds*
Rivers of Living Water
The Believer's #1 Need
The Bible Way to Spiritual Power
The Divine Flow*
The 6th Sense ... Faith
The Truth Shall Set You Free
There is a Miracle in Your Mouth*
This Awakening Generation
What to Do When the Tempter Comes
You Can Change Your Destiny

Mini-books:

A Place Called There
Four Principles in Receiving from God
How to Minister Healing to the Sick
Keep What God Gives
Love & Marriage
Receive the Holy Spirit
Saturday's Coming
ABC's of Faith
What to Do When Nothing Seems to Work

*Also available in Spanish

Order from:
John Osteen Publications
P. O. Box 23117
Houston, Texas 77228
(or from your local Christian Bookstore)

Reigning in Life as a King

John Osteen

A special thank you to

Betty Jackson

of Murfreesboro, Tennessee,
for her labor of love
in the production of
this book.

Contents

One

Reigning in Life by One, Jesus Christ

We may not be what we want to be, but thank God we are not what we used to be! We should not be critical of ourselves. We should not judge ourselves by the way we picture others.

> And from Jesus Christ, who is the faithful witness, and the first begotten of the dead, and the prince of the kings of the earth. Unto him that loved us, and washed us from our sins in his own blood,
>
> And hath made us kings and priests unto God and his Father; to him be glory and dominion for ever and ever. Amen.
>
> Revelation 1:5-6

God created man to be a king. The very moment you receive Jesus Christ as your Savior, you are made a KING and a PRIEST.

JESUS IS THE KING OF KINGS!

The Bible says that Jesus is the King of kings. Have you
ever wondered who the other kings are? You are one of
them. I am one of them. God intends for all Christians to
reign as kings.

Make this confession:

> I AM A KING.
> I REIGN IN LIFE AS A KING.

That is what God says about you.

> For if, because of one man's trespass (lapse, of-
> fense) death reigned through that one, much
> more surely will those who receive [God's] over-
> flowing grace (unmerited favor) and the free gift
> of righteousness (putting them into right stand-
> ing with Himself) reign as kings in life through
> the One, Jesus Christ, the Messiah, the
> Anointed One.
>
> Romans 5:17
> (Amplified)

Many times people say, "Let's just hold out to the end.
We may barely make it through this life. We may get to
heaven dressed in rags, but in the next life we will reign."

That is certainly not what Romans 5:17 means. The Apostle Paul said that death reigned in life through the offence
of Adam, but we which have received the abundance of
grace and the gift of righteousness are to reign in life
through Jesus Christ.

In the midst of trials,

In the midst of tribulations,

In the midst of the uncertainties of life,

In the midst of raising a family,

In the midst of all the problems that are hurled at us,

We are to live independent of circumstances, and REIGN AS KINGS!

You may say:

"I don't see it!"
You will see it.

"I can't make it!"
Well, you will.

"I don't understand it!"
You will understand it soon.

"I feel like a slave!"
You will feel differently.

You may have barely managed to get a copy of this book, but thank God you got one!

God has given you this book so that you can learn to reign victoriously over your circumstances even

in the midst of a broken home,

in the midst of divorce,

in the midst of the disappointments of life.

You should be so informed of your rights in Christ that you reign AS A KING in all situations.

> For if by one man's offence death reigned by
> one; much more they which receive abundance
> of grace and of the gift of righteousness shall
> reign in life by one, Jesus Christ.
>
> Romans 5:17

God has given us three great truths in this passage of
scripture.

First of all, it IS possible for us to reign in this life.

If we are not reigning in some areas, it is our own fault!
Whatever comes against us to overcome us is not God's
will. The Bible says we are to reign as kings in THIS life.

Second, we are to reign by One, Jesus Christ.

We cannot reign as kings in our own power. We must be
one with Christ. Since we reign by One, we only need to
be concerned about our relationship with Him. He makes
it possible for each of us to reign.

**Third, we reign in life because we have received an abun-
dance of grace and the gift of righteousness.**

If we do not understand grace and righteousness, we will
live under condemnation all our lives. That is a very sim-
ple statement, but to reign as kings we must understand
that we have received salvation through the abundant
grace of God, and not through our own works.

> For by grace are ye saved through faith; and
> that not of yourselves: it is the gift of God:

Not of works, lest any man should boast.

Ephesians 2:8-9

In the eyes of our Heavenly Father, we are as righteous as the Lord Jesus Christ! (II Corinthians 5:21)

WE ARE THE RIGHTEOUSNESS OF GOD.

Therefore, we will reign in this life as a king.

We are to reign as kings over
>   our bodies,
>
>   our carnal minds,
>
>   our homes,
>
>   our circumstances,
>
>   the atmosphere around us,
>
>   every demonic power,
>
>   every sickness and disease.

We are to reign over all the forces of darkness.

Many sons and daughters of God are actually living like slaves.

This fact stirs my heart to study, to pray, to develop my own spirit, and to change my thinking. I want to be able to help those who are living defeated lives because of their lack of knowledge.

Many children of God who should be reigning as kings in life are groveling in the dust as slaves, whipped by satanic powers. This ought not to be!

I want you to examine these scriptures with me.

The Spirit itself beareth witness with our spirit, that we are the children of God:

And if children, then heirs; heirs of God, and joint-heirs with Christ . . .
Romans 8:16-17a

Now I say, That the heir, as long as he is a child, differeth nothing from a servant, though he be lord of all.
Galatians 4:1

Make this confession boldly:

I AM AN HEIR.

I AM AN HEIR OF GOD.

I AM A JOINT-HEIR WITH JESUS.

You have been made lord of all by the great love of God.

There are three things that will keep you from KNOWING that you are lord of all:

1) Laziness

2) Indifference

3) Preoccupation with the world

If you continue as a child in your thinking, if you are uninformed in your spirit, if you are lazy and indifferent, if you are preoccupied with the things of the world, you will live as a servant. You will not function as a king in this life.

> Now we have received, not the spirit of the world, but the spirit which is of God; that we might know the things that are freely given to us of God.
>
> I Corinthians 2:12

Confess what the Bible says about you:

I HAVE THE SPIRIT OF GOD.

MY BODY IS THE TEMPLE OF THE HOLY GHOST.

Why do we have the Holy Ghost living within us? We have received the Spirit which is of God that we might KNOW the things that God has freely given to us.

The Holy Ghost dwells within us that we may understand the things of God. He wants to teach us the truths of the Word of God so that Satan will not be able to rob us of the blessings God has for us in this life. The Holy Ghost desires that we might fully know what God has provided for us. We should be constantly learning.

Near the end of his life, the Apostle Paul wrote to the Philippians:

> Yea doubtless, and I count all things but loss for the excellency of the knowledge of Christ Jesus my Lord: for whom I have suffered the

loss of all things, and do count them but dung,
that I may win Christ,

And be found in him, not having mine own
righteousness, which is of the law, but that
which is through the faith of Christ, the
righteousness which is of God by faith:

That I may know him, and the power of his
resurrection, and the fellowship of his suf-
ferings, being made conformable unto his death;

If by any means I might attain unto the resurrection of the dead.

Not as though I had already attained, either
were already perfect: but I follow after, if that
I may apprehend that for which also I am ap-
prehended of Christ Jesus.

Brethren, I count not myself to have apprehend-
ed: but this one thing I do, forgetting those
things which are behind, and reaching forth unto those things which are before,

I press toward the mark for the prize of the high
calling of God in Christ Jesus.

Philippians 3:8-14

FORGET THE PAST!

When you are born into the family of God, you are like
a newborn baby. You have no past. Your past sins and
failures are gone. Your sins and iniquities are remembered
no more. You are a new creature in Christ Jesus.

There is no past with God. Forget yesterday, and the

yesterday before that! Forget it! God has wiped it away!

PRESS IN TO KNOW HIM!

And I, brethren, could not speak unto you as
unto spiritual, but as unto carnal, even as unto
babes in Christ.

I Corinthians 3:1

This short passage of scripture tells us that there are three
kinds of Christians:

spiritual Christians,

carnal Christians,

baby Christians.

If a person acts like a baby and needs pampering, that
does not mean he is not a Christian. A new Christian is
often carnal because he has not yet learned many truths
from the Word of God.

There are spiritual Christians, carnal Christians, and baby
Christians. God will put up with babies, and give them
time to grow.

I have fed you with milk, and not with meat:
for hitherto ye were not able to bear it, neither
yet now are ye able.

For ye are yet carnal: for whereas there is
among you envying, and strife, and divisions,
are ye not carnal, and walk as men?

I Corinthians 3:2-3

Carnal Christians walk as men who are not ruled by the Spirit of God. This does not mean they are not Christians.

Many Christians are involved in questionable activities. That does not mean they have lost eternal life. It only indicates that they are worldly.

If we only knew the power of looking at something with our eyes, or hearing something with our ears, registering that in our brains, and sending it down to our spirits, we would be more careful to guard our eyes and our ears.

All kinds of blessings are available to those Christians who walk after the Spirit of God, and not after the flesh.

A close friend of ours shared with me a dream that the Lord had given her in the night. This dream came at a time when her family had great needs. They had not yet come to understand how to reign in life.

God revealed to her the most lovely banquet table, exquisitely set and filled with beautiful food. She sat down at her place, reached around all that luscious food, and pulled out a dry peanut butter and jelly sandwich to eat.

Then God gave her an understanding of the dream. God had provided far more for her family than they were taking. Now, she and her husband have learned how to reign as kings.

Many of us have heard from good Bible teachers what wonderful blessings God has available for us. Yet, some of us are such babies that we sit down and eat our peanut butter and jelly sandwiches. We go on complaining, driving our rattle traps, living in old dumps, and putting up with everything the devil throws at us.

It is time to throw down the peanut butter and jelly sandwich! Rise up in your spirit and declare:

I WILL REIGN AS A KING IN THIS LIFE!

Your enemy, the devil, rejoices over your lack of knowledge and every victory he gains over you.

Let us begin to confess that we do not have a lack of knowledge, and rejoice that we are victorious over the devil. The devil gets nervous when saints begin to understand who they are in Christ. God is developing an army of kings. If you want to remain a baby Christian or continue as a carnal Christian, that is up to you. I cannot make you become a king. However, I have made my decision!

I WILL REIGN AS A KING IN THIS LIFE!

God is preparing His kings. He is giving them intensive training. He is supplying and making them conscious of the weapons of their warfare.

In God's great kingdom, every king is not ready for battle. Everyone is not fully developed, but God is preparing us. He is teaching us that the weapons of our warfare are not carnal, but mighty through God to the pulling down of strongholds. (II Corinthians 10:4)

God allows us a training period. When we take hold of the

weapons that He has provided, we will surprise ourselves by what we can do. We will not need another Christian. We will not have to find someone else in the middle of the night. We can defeat the devil ourselves.

When you are in the midst of a battle, God will not automatically remove you from the fight just because you cry for help.

Suppose a bully at school had been threatening my son, Joel. What if I had taken time to teach him how to fight and defend himself. Then one day the bully picked on him and Joel began to yell, "Daddy, why don't you help me?"

Joel could win that battle. I had taught him how; but instead, he kept calling for help. Of course, I could walk in and stop the fight, but everything would remain the same. The bully would pick on him again.

On the other hand, if I just waited and let Joel realize I was not going to fight his battle, he would begin to remember his weapons. He would remember his training, and when he defeated that bully, things would change. He would know his own strength. He would know that he was the victor.

Many of us find ourselves in the battles of life and we say, "God will not hear me. Oh God, help, help, help!" We expect God to do something the very minute we get in trouble. If God did that, we would never become strong. God is not going to rescue us from every battle. He does not want us to remain baby Christians.

Several years ago I was believing God for two cows to supply the beef for our annual Thanksgiving Convention, but I gave up. I stopped believing for them. Later, God gave me a dream and I saw a field full of mammoth snakes. Two of those snakes had swallowed something, and as I looked closely, I saw the outline of a cow on the inside of each of them.

God said to me, "You let the devil swallow your two cows." I had lost that battle.

Another time I was going through a great battle. The devil attacked my mind, and fear came against me. This battle went on for months. It looked as if I were going to die. I thought, "Why doesn't God get me out of this?"

After nearly a year of suffering, I decided to spend time in the Word of God. I could hardly read the Bible because I was so nervous and tense, but I started. I stood up in my spirit, I read the Word, and I finally drove the enemy away from me.

God left me in that situation until I made up my mind to get into the Word of God and find out who I was, what I could do, and the power I had in the Name of Jesus.

I came out of the battle a much stronger individual. I will never be the same.

You say, "God does not hear me!"

Yes, He does! But, He is not going to instantly deliver you. He wants you to develop in your spirit. He has made you a king!

We have to understand that if God delivered us instantly, every time we asked, we would never develop an understanding of the authority He has given us.

> We have had some attacks.
> So what!
> Things are falling to pieces.
> So what!
> Everything is going wrong.
> So what!

God wants us to know who we are. He wants us to learn to use the Name of Jesus. He desires that we know the Word of God.

God wants us to defeat the enemy, to destroy his plans, and to come into the fullness of the knowledge of who we are in Christ Jesus. Yes, God wants us to stand up and change our situations and the circumstances of those around us.

In these last days, we must KNOW:

> We are not facing light skirmishes with foes that can be easily defeated.

> We are not fighting flesh and blood, or matching wits with men.

> We are being ambushed by spiritual forces.

> We are in open combat, facing Satan himself.

The devil is not just out to torment us. He is out to destroy us!

When we realize this, we will be eager to gain Biblical knowledge. We will rise early in the morning, take God's Word, and feed our spirits. When we realize the issues at stake, Bible study will become a must.

We will find God's people and begin to work together with them to fulfill the Great Commission before the return of the Lord Jesus Christ, our Lord of lords and King of kings!

Satan, knowing that he has but a short time, has great fury! He is trying to crush us! Unless we know who we are and what we can do by the power of Jesus Christ, Satan will have continuous victories in our lives.

I boldly declare:

> Satan has no part of me!
>
> The enemy has no power over me!
>
> I trample on serpents and scorpions!
>
> I am more than a conqueror!
>
> I reign in life as a king!

Without an understanding of the great redemptive truths of the Bible, we are no match for the devil. Alone, we cannot win. But by the power of what Jesus has done for us, every person reading this book can

REIGN IN LIFE AS A KING!

We do not have to be afraid of the devil! He trembles at the very sound of our footsteps.

Satan knows the spiritual hunger in people today. He trembles at the thought of men and women gaining a knowledge of who they are in Christ Jesus!

We cannot expect God to continue to instantly rescue us when we cry out in distress. We must learn to take God's Word and fight our way out! God wants us to stay in the arena until we defeat the devil.

The Father will say, "Jesus, there is one of Your kings!"

Then we will be prepared to be sent by the Lord Jesus on strategic missions. When we are reigning as kings in life, He knows that we will be faithful. God is looking for a people He can trust. He wants to use us to bring millions of souls to Himself.

The Apostle Paul reigned in life by One, Jesus Christ. When he was on board a ship, headed for Rome, he was a prisoner in chains, but he had a divine revelation from God. The other men on that ship did not know they had a king on board. Even though they could bind Paul's hands, they could not bind the power of God in his life.

I can imagine the devil and his demons saying, "Look! I thought he was a powerful Christian!" They did not recognize who he was or what he could do.

However, Paul knew who he was. Getting on board the ship, he said, "You should not sail!", but they sailed anyway.

Soon they were in a terrible storm. They were driven night

and day by the winds, and could see neither the sun nor stars for many days. All hope was gone. Here was one of God's great kings in chains. His outward circumstances were bad. Nothing can be worse than to have all hope gone.

> But after long abstinence Paul stood forth in the midst of them, and said, Sirs, ye should have hearkened unto me, and not have loosed from Crete, and to have gained this harm and loss.
>
> And now I exhort you to be of good cheer: for there shall be no loss of any man's life among you, but of the ship.
>
> For there stood by me this night the angel of God, whose I am, and whom I serve,
>
> Saying, Fear not, Paul; thou must be brought before Caesar: and, lo, God hath given thee all them that sail with thee.
>
> Wherefore, sirs, be of good cheer: for I believe God, that it shall be even as it was told me.
>
> Acts 27:21-25

They thought Paul was sailing with THEM. They thought he was a prisoner, but he was a king. Paul was an ambassador, and in God's eyes, they were sailing with HIM. Everything revolved around the king!

If it looks like all hope is gone, take heart!

Do not give up!

Do not write off your child!

Do not write off your mate!

Do not write off your family!

If you have chosen to be a king, all hope is NOT gone.

I want you to say:

I AM A KING!

I REIGN IN LIFE BY ONE, JESUS CHRIST!

> And as the shipmen were about to flee out of
> the ship, when they had let down the boat into
> the sea, under colour as though they would have
> cast anchors out of the foreship,
>
> Paul said to the centurion and to the soldiers,
> Except these abide in the ship, ye cannot be
> saved.
>
> Acts 27:30-31

Paul went on board a slave in their eyes. They refused to
listen to him, but he knew who he was, and now he was
in charge. When those crew members started to jump over-
board, he said, "No, do not let them jump!" He gave the
orders and they did exactly as he said.

God's king may have been chained, but in the end all could
see that he was reigning!

Do you know why Paul reigned? He said, "For I believe
God, that it shall be even as it was told me."

God has told us in His Word that we are healed by the
stripes of Jesus. (I Peter 2:24)

God also said that He would supply all our needs. (Philippians 4:19)

Kings stand up in the face of every storm and declare: "The Bible says it, therefore, it must come to pass!" Kings go by what is told them in the Book of the kings!

God wants us to stay in the fight until we know that we can defeat the devil!

We must know the power in the Name of Jesus so that we can drive the enemy forces from the field of battle!

God wants us to stand as more than conquerors:

undaunted,

unflinching,

unshaken,

unafraid!

God wants us to stand as kings in the powerful Name of Jesus!

WE REIGN IN LIFE AS KINGS BY ONE,
JESUS CHRIST.

Two

Reigning in Life Through Our Exalted Position in Christ

> And from Jesus Christ, who is the faithful witness, and the first begotten of the dead, and the prince of the kings of the earth. Unto him that loved us, and washed us from our sins in his own blood,
>
> And hath made us kings and priests unto God and his Father; to him be glory and dominion for ever and ever. Amen.
>
> Revelation 1:5-6

Thank God, the Apostle John did not say that Jesus was trying to make us, hoped to make us, or was in the process of making us kings and priests.

He said, "Jesus HATH made us kings and priests unto God and His Father."

> For if by one man's offence death reigned by one; much more they which receive abundance of grace and of the gift of righteousness shall

reign in life by one, Jesus Christ.

Romans 5:17

Have you received an abundance of grace? Have you received the gift of righteousness? If you have, God declares in His Word that YOU SHALL REIGN IN LIFE.

Make it a priority in your life to remember each day:

GOD HAS MADE YOU A KING.

We are to reign even if:

we have battles,

we go through many hard places,

and problems come against us.

God intended for us to be overcomers in all of these things. He wants to train us to reign over every circumstance IN THIS PRESENT LIFE.

Most of us understand and believe that we will reign in the next life.

> And Jesus said unto them, Verily I say unto you, That ye which have followed me, in the regeneration when the Son of man shall sit in the throne of his glory, ye also shall sit upon twelve thrones, judging the twelve tribes of Israel.
>
> Matthew 19:28

Jesus was speaking to His twelve disciples. He said that they were going to reign and judge as kings. You may be thinking, "That does not say I am going to reign!" Let's read the words of Paul.

> Dare any of you, having a matter against another, go to law before the unjust, and not before the saints?
>
> Do ye not know that the saints shall judge the world? and if the world shall be judged by you, are ye unworthy to judge the smallest matters?
>
> Know ye not that we shall judge angels? how much more things that pertain to this life?
>
> I Corinthians 6:1-3

Our court system has its basis in the Old Testament. It is an integral part of our society in settling disputes. In dealing with the world, Christians may have to use the courts that God ordained, but we should not have to go to court with another Christian. We have the Word of God to help judge our situations. God even instructs us to lose something for the sake of another brother.

Christian couples who are facing a divorce should sit down with a brother or sister who understands repentance and forgiveness, and by the Word of God judge the situation. Instead of divorce, there can be victory; love and harmony can be gained, and the marriage restored.

There is no question about the fact that we will reign in heaven. We will also have a part in the judgment. Therefore, there is no reason for God's children to fear the judgment.

The Word of God also says that we can REIGN IN THIS
PRESENT LIFE. God does not want us to see ourselves
as slaves.

> Now I say, That the heir, as long as he is a child,
> differeth nothing from a servant, though he be
> lord of all.
>
> Galatians 4:1

It is not enough to be an heir. We must KNOW and
UNDERSTAND what it means to be an heir.

Make this confession:

> I AM AN HEIR OF GOD.
>
> I AM A JOINT-HEIR WITH JESUS CHRIST.

Even though we are heirs and lords over all things, as long
as we remain children, we will continue to walk and act
like servants.

Many people will live, die, and meet Jesus, never having
entered into what their Heavenly Father intended for them
to have because they are:

> worldly,
>
> carnal,
>
> babies,
>
> unspiritual,
>
> undeveloped in their spirits.

You should not remain a baby Christian. You can grow up. You can mature. You can come to the realization of what it means to be an heir of God. You do not have to walk through life as a servant. You do not have to be overcome by circumstances and demonic powers!

YOU CAN BE LORD IN THIS LIFE
THROUGH JESUS CHRIST!

In order to reign in life, we need KNOWLEDGE.

I have been in services where I have been worked into a frenzy by a good sermon. I wanted to run and shout. However, when I wiped off the perspiration, I could not remember much of what I had heard or why I was so happy!

It is good to be inspired, but we cannot live on inspiration. We have tried for years, but the time has come for us to be informed of what God says in His Word.

It is better to know one verse of scripture, meditate on it, make it our own, and act on it, than to have all the inspiration in the world.

One time I put twenty dollars in the secret compartment of my wallet. My wife, Dodie, did not know I had it. I thought I would use it for an emergency. There were several occasions when I needed cash, but I had forgotten about the twenty dollar bill. I had what I needed, but I lacked a KNOWLEDGE of it.

We need to KNOW what God has done for us. We need

to KNOW what God has made available to us.

One day the local newspaper carried an article about a man's death. He was a beggar who had walked up and down the streets eating trash out of garbage cans. He died in a little hovel. When they examined his body, they found a money belt around him that contained twenty-eight thousand dollars. He had been eating out of garbage cans!

It is not enough to have knowledge. We must be willing to put that knowledge to use.

There are many Christians walking around with millions of dollars worth of truth in their hearts, but they have never opened their mouths. They have never taken their stand on the Word of God. They have never done one thing about their condition. They continue to eat out of garbage cans even though they have knowledge. Oh, if they would only act on the knowledge they have!

Some Christians say, "The devil is after me. Help me, help me!" They have a wealth of truth at their disposal, but they are eating out of a garbage can.

Others say, "I'm afraid!" They are eating out of the garbage can of fear. They could use the Name of the Lord Jesus Christ and resist that fear.

> And these signs shall follow them that believe;
> In my name shall they cast out devils...
>
> Mark 16:17a

We need to stand up and chase the devil away!

There have been untold legions of demonic spirits unleashed upon this world. The whole world lies in darkness. The very atmosphere is filled with demonic powers and unclean spirits. There are organized rulerships in the atmosphere about us. There is an assigned, demonic prince over each of the nations of the world.

The work of demons is not just to vex us, or to harrass us. The devil wants to destroy us and drag us into hell, but he cannot do that! We will not let him!

The Bible says we are to reign as KINGS in this life. God did not intend for us to subject ourselves to these demonic powers and circumstances. He did not intend for us to barely get along in life.

WE MUST KNOW WHO WE ARE IN CHRIST.

WE ARE TO HOLD UP OUR HEADS.

WE ARE TO REIGN AS KINGS IN THIS LIFE.

We are to take charge in adverse circumstances and drive the devil away from us! When evil surrounds us, the very atmosphere around us can be charged with the power of the Name of Jesus.

You may find yourself in a situation where you are surrounded by depression. Your house may be filled with depression. You can change that atmosphere!

YOU ARE A KING IN THIS LIFE.

You can stop depression in your home. Say, "Wait a

minute! We are not going to say anything unless we can
say something good. We are going to fill this house with
the glory of God and with the praises of the Lord Jesus
Christ because we reign in life!"

On the Day of Pentecost the scripture says that those who
heard Peter's sermon were pricked in their hearts, and they
posed the question, "What shall we do?" Peter answered
with three things for them to do:

1) Repent.

2) Be baptized for the remission of sins.

3) Receive the gift of the Holy Ghost.

According to the Book of Acts, when the church began
on the Day of Pentecost, three thousand people acted on
these three truths at one time. They simply obeyed Peter's
words.

> In whom ye also trusted, after that ye heard the
> word of truth, the gospel of your salvation: in
> whom also after that ye believed, ye were
> sealed with that holy Spirit of promise,
>
> Which is the earnest of our inheritance until the
> redemption of the purchased possession, unto
> the praise of his glory.
>   Ephesians 1:13-14

In the Book of Ephesians, Paul was writing to believers.
These were Christians who had been baptized in the Holy
Spirit.

Paul told the Ephesians that five things had already been

accomplished in them:

1) They heard the Gospel.

2) They believed the Gospel.

3) They trusted Jesus Christ as Savior.

4) They were sealed with the Holy Spirit.

5) They had become God's purchased possession.

Wherefore I also, after I heard of your faith in the Lord Jesus, and love unto all the saints,

Cease not to give thanks for you, making mention of you in my prayers;

That the God of our Lord Jesus Christ, the Father of glory, may give unto you the spirit of wisdom and revelation in the knowledge of him:

The eyes of your understanding being enlightened; that ye may know what is the hope of his calling, and what the riches of the glory of his inheritance in the saints,

And what is the exceeding greatness of his power to us-ward who believe, according to the working of his mighty power,

Which he wrought in Christ, when he raised him from the dead, and set him at his own right hand in the heavenly places,

Far above all principality, and power, and might, and dominion, and every name that is named, not only in this world, but also in that which is to come:

> And hath put all things under his feet, and gave
> him to be the head over all things to the church.
>
> Ephesians 1:15-22

Paul prayed that God would give the Ephesian believers a spirit of wisdom and revelation in the knowledge of Him.

Evidently, receiving Jesus and being baptized in the Holy Spirit does not automatically give us this revelation. If it did, Paul would not have been making this request of God.

Believing is not the ultimate purpose that God has for our lives.

GOD WANTS US TO HAVE KNOWLEDGE.

Believing leads to KNOWING. Prompted by the Holy Spirit, Paul prayed that the church at Ephesus would come to KNOW three things.

First, Paul prayed that the believers would know the hope of their calling.

Hope is an assurance, a confident expectation of the future. God wants us to have a confident expectation of what lies ahead of us both in time and in eternity.

The final hope of the Christian in this life is the blessed appearing of our Lord Jesus and spending eternity with Him.

Second, Paul prayed that the Ephesians would know the riches of the glory of God's inheritance in the saints.

Our Father paid a terrific price for each of us. The minute we accept Jesus, we become God's property! We become His own. We have been purchased back by our Creator. We are His inheritance.

God wants to produce in us A MASTERPIECE OF FAITH, a holy character. He wants to make us like Himself!

We must realize that we are valuable to God.

Third, Paul prayed that they would know the power that is available to those who believe.

There is only one basic requirement for having God's power available in our lives. That requirement is BELIEVING. God's power is available as we believe.

Consider for a moment that this power, which is in us, is the SAME POWER that raised the dead body of Jesus from the tomb and took it into the presence of God.

That same power is available to every one of us who believes. This power will no longer be hidden from us when we receive the spirit of wisdom and revelation in the knowledge of God.

> And you hath he quickened, who were dead in trespasses and sins;
>
> Wherein in time past ye walked according to the course of this world, according to the prince of the power of the air, the spirit that now worketh in the children of disobedience:

Among whom also we all had our conversation
in times past in the lusts of our flesh, fulfilling
the desires of the flesh and of the mind; and
were by nature the children of wrath, even as
others.

But God, who is rich in mercy, for his great love
wherewith he loved us,

Even when we were dead in sins, hath quick-
ened us together with Christ, (by grace ye are
saved;)

And hath raised us up together, and made us
sit together in heavenly places in Christ Jesus:

That in the ages to come he might shew the exceeding riches of his grace in his kindness
toward us through Christ Jesus.

Ephesians 2:1-7

Pray this prayer with me:

Heavenly Father, I come to Your great
throne of mercy, boldly confessing Your
Word.

I know that You are my Father.

I know that Jesus is my Lord, my Savior,
my Great Redeemer!

I know that the Holy Spirit dwells within
my body.

All my sins are forgiven, through the blood
of Jesus.

I thank You, Father, that I have obeyed

Your Word, and I have forgiven every one who has ever wronged me. I have forgiven myself.

Father, You have forgiven my sins. You have forgotten them. My sins are under the blood of Jesus. Now, I will forget them.

Heavenly Father, I thank You that through the Name of Jesus, You have given me a spirit of wisdom and revelation in the knowledge of Him.

Father, because of the knowledge You have given me, I know how great is the hope to which You have called me. Your Word says that You are rich because of me. How tremendous is the power available to us who believe.

I praise You, Father, that while I was dead in sin, You made me alive. You raised me up.

I thank You, Father, that You have seated me beside You in heavenly places, far above all principalities and powers. Through the ages to come, use me to demonstrate the immeasurable riches of Your free grace.

Through your exalted position in Christ, YOU ARE LOOKING DOWN! You are FAR ABOVE all principalities and powers. All things are under your feet. You are seated in heavenly places in Christ Jesus.

You will reign in this life as a king because you have this KNOWLEDGE.

Confess boldly:

> I know my sins are forgiven.
>
> I know they are remembered against me
> no more.
>
> I know I am the righteousness of God in
> Christ Jesus.
>
> I know I am seated with Christ.
>
> I REIGN IN LIFE AS A KING!

Now when demonic powers come against you, do not be afraid.

> You may have a struggle with drinking.
>
> You may be tempted to take drugs.
>
> You may be involved in witchcraft.
>
> You may have an uncontrollable temper.
>
> You may have a sickness or disease.

You do not have to be afraid of any of these things!

First say, "I am going to look down." Then you will realize your position in Christ. You are seated in heavenly places and you have power over the devil.

> Behold, I give unto you power to tread on
> serpents and scorpions, and over all the power
> of the enemy: and nothing shall by any means
> hurt you.
>
>   Luke 10:19

The devil and all his demon forces are under your feet.

> Neither give place to the devil.
>
> Ephesians 4:27

Even though the Word of God teaches us to give no place to the devil, many people have given him a place equal to themselves in spiritual power. Many people think the devil has great power.

Satan's power is limited to how much place we give him in our lives. God does not want us to be overcome by wicked spirits that have already been defeated by Jesus. He does not want us held in bondage to them.

WE ARE EXALTED IN CHRIST!

We have an exalted position in Christ. We are seated together with Him in heavenly places. We can reign in this life through Jesus Christ!

Read what Jesus says about you.

> Ye are the light of the world. A city that is set
> on an hill cannot be hid.
>
> Matthew 5:14

God will not have to search for us because we are shining as lights. We are reigning in the kingdom of light! The world is in darkness, but we are not of the world. We are the light that is in the world.

> Herein is our love made perfect, that we may

have boldness in the day of judgment: because
as he is, so are we in this world.

1 John 4:17

We are like Jesus in this world.

Jesus is exalted.

Jesus is above all powers.

Jesus is victorious.

Jesus is a King.

God intended for us to be like Jesus in this world!

God does not always deliver us immediately from trouble. We must use the weapons that He has provided for
us and defeat the devil ourselves. God wants us to develop
and mature as Christians, and learn to stay on the field
of battle until we win.

Yes, we may get knocked down. Yes, we may feel we are
losing ground. We may even suffer some defeats, but one
day we will shake ourselves and say, "Wait a minute! I
do not have to put up with this anymore."

I HAVE AN EXALTED POSITION IN CHRIST!

I REIGN IN LIFE BY ONE, JESUS CHRIST!

When you have had enough of the devil and all of his
schemes, you will take the Word of God and drive the
enemy away from you and your family.

Once you have taken this exalted position, you will never

be the same! You may be surrounded by adverse circumstances, but you can change that atmosphere. Take charge. Do not be afraid! You will pass the test. Stand up tall and say:

> Satan, you are looking at a king!
>
> I bear the Name of Jesus!
>
> I am covered with the blood of Jesus!
>
> My attendants are the mighty angels of God!
>
> I am filled with the Spirit of God!
>
> Get out of my way!
>
> I REIGN IN LIFE BY ONE, JESUS CHRIST!

In Acts, Chapter Twenty-seven, Paul was on board a ship as a prisoner, but it was not long until he was in charge. He knew who he was. He had KNOWLEDGE. In the midst of the terrible storm, Paul told the men to be of good cheer because every person would be spared.

Sometimes you may feel chained. If you will remember WHO YOU ARE, you will soon be in charge again.

All hope was gone for Paul and the others on that ship, but Paul knew what God had told him. He stood on the Word of God and the situation changed! Every person aboard that ship was saved.

As soon as the men were safe from the shipwreck, they placed Paul back in the position of a prisoner. They told him to collect the wood for a fire. He had just saved their lives, but now they said, "Get out and pick up the sticks!"

The devil was watching. He had failed to kill Paul in the storm. Now he thought, "While these servants of mine have him gathering sticks, I will send a snake to destroy him."

> And when Paul had gathered a bundle of sticks, and laid them on the fire, there came a viper out of the heat, and fastened on his hand.
>
> And when the barbarians saw the venomous beast hang on his hand, they said among themselves, No doubt this man is a murderer, whom, though he hath escaped the sea, yet vengeance suffereth not to live.
>
> And he shook off the beast into the fire, and felt no harm.
>
> Howbeit they looked when he should have swollen, or fallen down dead suddenly: but after they had looked a great while, and saw no harm come to him, they changed their minds, and said that he was a god.
>
> Acts 28:3-6

Paul did not mind gathering the branches. He was not afraid of an attack of the devil. When that snake attached itself to his hand, the kingdom of God inside Paul began to manifest. Kings who walk in the knowledge of their position in Christ do not swell up and die!

When we have this knowledge, it takes more than all the forces of hell to kill us. It does not matter if we are chained, or made to pick up sticks. If we have knowledge, we will reign in life through Jesus Christ!

When Paul did not swell up and die, they decided he was a god. The hands that had picked up sticks were used to heal the sick. The whole island recognized a KING!

When we know who we are, we do not mind picking up sticks. We do face battles and sometimes it seems as if flood tides of evil have come against us, but we must not give up! Kings do not mind fighting the battle when they know the end is victory. When God gives us a promise, He will bring it to pass!

WE REIGN IN LIFE AS KINGS
THROUGH OUR EXALTED POSITION IN CHRIST.

Three

Reigning in Life Through the Abundance of Grace

Paul explains his position in a beautiful way in his letter to the Corinthians. He confessed to them that he was the least of the apostles because he had persecuted the Church. Paul knew that he could not boast in himself, but neither did he have anything of which to be ashamed.

> But by the grace of God I am what I am: and his grace which was bestowed upon me was not in vain; but I laboured more abundantly than they all: yet not I, but the grace of God which was with me.
>
> I Corinthians 15:10

Sometimes we tend to think that everything depends entirely upon us and what we can do. As a result, we become frustrated and disappointed with our lives. If Paul had considered his past, he would have been discouraged. But he was able to say, "By the grace of God I am what I am!"

> For if by one man's offence death reigned by one; much more they which receive abundance

of grace and of the gift of righteousness shall
reign in life by one, Jesus Christ.

Romans 5:17

The word *grace* appears approximately forty times in the
Old Testament and one hundred and fifty times in the New
Testament. Grace is undeserved favor. It is the founda-
tion of the Christian life.

When Paul greeted the churches, he began by saying,
"Grace be unto you, and peace from God our Father, and
from the Lord Jesus Christ." Usually, he closed his letters by writing, "The grace of our Lord Jesus Christ be
with you." Paul knew that the believers needed the grace
of God to live out the Gospel in their daily lives.

God created Adam to reign in life, and He gave him dominion over all the earth. He gave Adam a free will, or the
power of choice. Then, God put something in the garden
to allow him to exercise that power of choice. The choice
was whether to obey or to disobey God. When Adam
sinned, death reigned on this earth.

God has given every man and woman the power of choice.
We can choose to believe God's Word, or we can choose
to believe a lie of Satan.

Satan came in the form of a beautiful serpent to tempt
Eve. Today, he comes to tempt people in many different
areas. He may even come as an angel of light. (II Corinthians 11:14)

The moment Adam lost his authority and dominion, the

great love of God began to act on behalf of all mankind. God never intended for man to go through life under the authority of Satan or any of his demon forces. God told Satan that He would break his lordship through the seed of a woman, and that He would use man to bruise his head.

> And the Lord God said unto the serpent, Because thou hast done this, thou art cursed above all cattle, and above every beast of the field; upon thy belly shalt thou go, and dust shalt thou eat all the days of thy life:
>
> And I will put enmity between thee and the woman, and between thy seed and her seed; it shall bruise thy head, and thou shalt bruise his heel.
>
> Genesis 3:14-15

Jesus defeated Satan and then He said to us:

> Behold, I give unto you power to tread on serpents and scorpions, and over all the power of the enemy: and nothing shall by any means hurt you.
>
> Luke 10:19

In Genesis we read that as man began to multiply on the face of the earth, God saw that the wickedness of man was great in the earth, and his thoughts were continually evil. (Genesis 6:5)

> And the Lord said, I will destroy man whom I have created from the face of the earth; both man, and beast, and the creeping thing, and the

> fowls of the air; for it repenteth me that I have
> made them.
>
> Genesis 6:7

God knows what is in a man's heart. He knows our thoughts. (Psalm 139:2)

Throughout the Bible, we learn that God looks at His people through eyes of grace. God looks at our hearts. (Proverbs 21:2) He knows our motives, and when no one else can see anything attractive about us, He begins to move on our behalf.

Have you ever considered a field of grass in the winter months? It is usually brown and unattractive—very insignificant. In fact, you could pass that field day after day and not even notice it.

In the springtime, when the rains fall and the sun begins to shine on that field, the grass turns green and it becomes a lush pasture land. The cattle begin to eat the grass and bear their young. Soon little calves skip around their mothers, enjoying life.

That field is an example of the grace of God. You can be an insignificant businessman or housewife—someone the world has never noticed. Then God looks at you. The Son begins to shine upon you, and you not only become attractive to God, but to those around you. You begin to reproduce. You begin to bear fruit.

> For the eyes of the Lord run to and fro
> throughout the whole earth, to shew himself
> strong in the behalf of them whose heart is

perfect toward him.

> II Chronicles 16:9a

Noah's life was a demonstration of the grace of God.

> But Noah found grace in the eyes of the Lord.

> These are the generations of Noah: Noah was
> a just man and perfect in his generations, and
> Noah walked with God.
>> Genesis 6:8-9

Noah had been a preacher of righteousness. He was unnoticed by his generation, but not unnoticed by God. The eyes of the Lord rested upon Noah, and he began to hear God speak to him. Noah began to obey the voice of God.

Abraham found favor in the eyes of the Lord.

> And he lift up his eyes and looked, and, lo, three
> men stood by him: and when he saw them, he
> ran to meet them from the tent door, and
> bowed himself toward the ground,

> And said, My Lord, if now I have found favour
> in thy sight, pass not away, I pray thee, from
> thy servant.
>> Genesis 18:2-3

The eyes of the Lord rested on Abraham, and he began to hear God speak to him.

> And I will make thee exceeding fruitful, and I
> will make nations of thee, and kings shall come
> out of thee.

> And I will establish my covenant between me
> and thee and thy seed after thee in their genera-
> tions for an everlasting covenant, to be a God
> unto thee, and to thy seed after thee.
>
> Genesis 17:6-7

We are the seed of Abraham. God's covenant with
Abraham is our covenant. When God looked at Abraham,
He not only saw Abraham, He saw you and me. God saw
us reigning in life as kings.

> And if ye be Christ's, then are ye Abraham's
> seed, and heirs according to the promise.
>
> Galatians 3:29

The life of Joseph beautifully exemplifies the grace of God.

Joseph was born the eleventh son of His father, Jacob.
He was his favorite child, being born when Jacob was ninety years old. The father's favoritism aroused the envy of
the older brothers until they sold Joseph into slavery.

As a young slave in Egypt, Joseph was soon discovered
by Potiphar, an officer of Pharoah, who gave him charge
of all his house.

> And the Lord was with Joseph, and he was a
> prosperous man; and he was in the house of his
> master the Egyptian.
>
> And his master saw that the Lord was with him,
> and that the Lord made all that he did to pros-
> per in his hand.

> And Joseph found grace in his sight, and he
> served him: and he made him overseer over his
> house, and all that he had he put into his hand.

Genesis 39:2-4

Due to false accusations, Joseph was put in prison, but he soon gained the confidence of the jailor, and eventually all the prisoners were committed to his charge.

God enabled Joseph to interpret prophetic dreams for Pharoah. Then, God gave him the wisdom to recommend a plan for the salvation of Egypt. God told him how to save produce for the coming years of famine. Joseph was placed in charge of the royal granaries and was made an official next in rank to the king himself.

The famine came as Joseph had predicted and it affected the whole world. God had placed Joseph in a position to provide food for his brothers who had sold him into slavery.

When his brothers came to Egypt to buy grain, Joseph was their only supply. He forgave his brothers and invited them to live in the land of Egypt.

Joseph, his brothers, and all that generation died, but the Israelites were fruitful and multiplied greatly so that the land was filled with them.

Then a new king, who did not know Joseph, came to power in Egypt. He feared their number and put slave masters over all the Israelites. The more they were oppressed, the more they multiplied and spread. Eventually, the edict came—every newborn boy was to be thrown into the river, but every newborn girl could live.

Before his death, Joseph had spoken a promise to his brothers.

> And Joseph said unto his brethren, I die: and God will surely visit you, and bring you out of this land unto the land which he sware to Abraham, to Isaac, and to Jacob.
>
> Genesis 50:24

The Psalmist said of the Lord:

> The eyes of the Lord are upon the righteous, and his ears are open unto their cry.
>
> Psalm 34:15

When God encourages His people to seek His face, He is urging them to live in such a way that His eyes can be turned in their direction. This is what happened to the children of Israel. God heard their cry.

At this time, Moses was born, and his mother hid him for three months in order to save his life. When she could no longer hide him, she placed him in an ark of bulrushes and put him among the reeds on the river's bank.

He was taken by the king's daughter to the palace and his own mother became his nurse. Being the adopted son of a princess of a nation that was unsurpassed in civilization by any people in the world at that time, Moses was instructed in all the wisdom of the Egyptians.

Years later, Moses visited his own people and observed them in bondage of slavery. He saw an Egyptian beating a Hebrew, one of his own people, and in anger, he killed the Egyptian and hid him in the sand.

When Pharoah heard this, he tried to kill Moses, but Moses fled to Midian. There he lived for forty years learning the ways of the wilderness, its resources, and its climate. God was preparing Moses to spend the next forty years in the wilderness with the Israelites. It was here that he saw the burning bush and the Lord spoke to him.

> And the Lord said, I have surely seen the affliction of my people which are in Egypt, and have heard their cry by reason of their taskmasters; for I know their sorrows;
>
> And I am come down to deliver them out of the hand of the Egyptians, and to bring them up out of that land unto a good land and a large, unto a land flowing with milk and honey. . .
>
> Exodus 3:7-8a

God gave specific instructions through Moses for each household of Israel to sacrifice one spotless lamb and to place the blood of that lamb on the doorpost of their house. The blood of the lamb was a sign for the death angel to pass over that house. This sacrifice is known as the Passover.

> And the blood shall be to you for a token upon the houses where ye are: and when I see the blood, I will pass over you, and the plague shall

not be upon you to destroy you, when I smite
the land of Egypt.

> Exodus 12:13

God, through Moses, brought deliverance to His people.

The Lord Jesus Christ came to earth and offered Himself
as our sacrificial Lamb. It was at the Cross, the shedding
of the blood of the spotless Lamb of God, where the grace
of God was offered not to one man, not to one nation, but
to all who would receive Him.

> But God's free gift is not at all to be compared
> to the trespass—His grace is out of all propor-
> tion to the fall of man. For if many died through
> one man's falling away—his lapse, his
> offense—much more profusely did God's grace
> and the free gift [that comes] through the
> undeserved favor of the one Man Jesus Christ,
> abound and overflow to and for [the benefit of]
> many.
>
> Romans 5:15
> (Amplified)

The Bible teaches us that all men died spiritually when
Adam sinned. God, through Jesus Christ, brings life to
all who will receive Him. His grace is out of all propor-
tion to the fall of man. The first Adam was made a living
soul; the last Adam (Jesus) was made a life-giving Spirit.

> For if by one man's offence death reigned by
> one; much more they which receive abundance
> of grace and of the gift of righteousness shall
> reign in life by one, Jesus Christ.
>
> Romans 5:17

Through the grace of God, we have received the Spirit of Christ. We are no longer dead in trespasses and sins. We have received an abundance of grace.

> For the grace of God that bringeth salvation hath appeared to all men.
>
> Titus 2:11

The Prophet Jeremiah foretold the restoration of God's people. He could see the Church of Jesus Christ through eyes of faith.

> For I will set mine eyes upon them for good, and I will bring them again to this land: and I will build them, and not pull them down; and I will plant them, and not pluck them up.
>
> And I will give them an heart to know me, that I am the Lord: and they shall be my people, and I will be their God: for they shall return unto me with their whole heart.
>
> Jeremiah 24:6-7

God has looked upon His Church, and we have found grace in His sight! The Prophet Isaiah also saw the glory of the Church.

> As for me, this is my covenant with them, saith the Lord; My spirit that is upon thee, and my words which I have put in thy mouth, shall not depart out of thy mouth, nor out of the mouth of thy seed, nor out of the mouth of thy seed's seed, saith the Lord, from henceforth and for ever.
>
> Isaiah 59:21

Arise, shine; for thy light is come, and the glory
of the Lord is risen upon thee.

For, behold, the darkness shall cover the earth,
and gross darkness the people: but the Lord
shall arise upon thee, and his glory shall be seen
upon thee.

                                                    Isaiah 60:1-2

Isaiah prophesied that there would come forth a stem of
Jesse and the Spirit of the Lord would rest upon Him:

the spirit of wisdom,

the spirit of understanding,

the spirit of counsel,

the spirit of might,

the spirit of knowledge,

and the fear of the Lord.

Isaiah said that Jesus, this stem of Jesse, would not judge
after the sight of His eyes, neither reprove after the hearing of His ears. (Isaiah 11:1-4) God sent Jesus into the
world that we might be like Him. He is our perfect example. He dwelt among us that we might know Him.

He came unto his own, and his own received him
not.

But as many as received him, to them gave he
power to become the sons of God, even to them
that believe on his name:

Which were born, not of blood, nor of the will

of the flesh, nor of the will of man, but of God.

John 1:11-13

And of his fulness have all we received, and grace for grace.

For the law was given by Moses, but grace and truth came by Jesus Christ.

John 1:16-17

By the grace of God that came through Jesus Christ, we have the power to become the sons of God. We can be led by the Spirit of God. We can have the spirit of wisdom, understanding, counsel, might, knowledge, and the fear of the Lord. We do not have to judge after what our eyes see or our ears hear. Our direction comes from within us—through the Spirit of God who resides in our spirits.

THE GRACE OF GOD IS FREE!

We cannot earn it. We cannot work for it. We can never make ourselves acceptable to God. We must receive His grace through faith and come to God as we are. The Bible teaches us that while we were dead in sin, Jesus made us alive. A dead man cannot work! A dead man cannot earn anything.

But God, who is rich in mercy, for his great love wherewith he loved us,

Even when we were dead in sins, hath quick-ened us together with Christ, (by grace ye are saved;)

> And hath raised us up together, and made us
> sit together in heavenly places in Christ Jesus:
>
> That in the ages to come he might shew the ex-
> ceeding riches of his grace in his kindness
> toward us through Christ Jesus.
>
> For by grace are ye saved through faith; and
> that not of yourselves: it is the gift of God:
>
> Not of works, lest any man should boast.
>
> Ephesians 2:4-9

We are saved by grace through faith, that is, by believing that salvation is a free gift.

Grace is a gift of God. We cannot boast about it!

Grace originates with God. It cannot be achieved by
works.

> Now to him that worketh is the reward not
> reckoned of grace, but of debt.
>
> But to him that worketh not, but believeth on
> him that justifieth the ungodly, his faith is
> counted for righteousness.
> Romans 4:4-5

We must stop working to be justified and start believing
that we ARE justified! That is when God counts us
righteous.

When we receive Jesus Christ, we receive the total grace
of God. In every situation in which we realize we need
grace, Jesus is the Source.

We are no match for the devil in our own strength. Our emotions are not the tool with which we defeat the devil.

God's grace begins where our ability ends. When the situation is impossible, if you will believe, you will see the grace of God manifested.

If you are tempted to be angry, allow Jesus to demonstrate His peace. (Colossians 3:15) If you are tempted to doubt, remember the life you now live is by faith in Him. (Galatians 2:20) If you are tempted to give up, believe that you have His strength to go on. (Philippians 4:13)

HIS GRACE IS ALWAYS SUFFICIENT!

> For this thing I besought the Lord thrice, that it might depart from me.
>
> And he said unto me, My grace is sufficient for thee: for my strength is made perfect in weakness. Most gladly therefore will I rather glory in my infirmities, that the power of Christ may rest upon me.
>
> Therefore I take pleasure in infirmities, in reproaches, in necessities, in persecutions, in distresses for Christ's sake: for when I am weak, then am I strong.
>
> II Corinthians 12:8-10

Should we not say as Paul said, "I take pleasure in the midst of my need because I know that His grace is sufficient. God will meet my needs whether they are spiritual, mental, physical, marital, or financial. Not only will He meet my needs, but through this experience I will gain confidence in knowing Him.''

> And God is able to make all grace abound
> toward you; that ye, always having all sufficiency in all things, may abound to every good
> work.
>   II Corinthians 9:8

There is no insufficiency in Jesus. His grace is sufficient in all circumstances.

WE REIGN IN LIFE AS KINGS
THROUGH THE ABUNDANCE OF GRACE.

Four

Reigning in Life Through the Gift of Righteousness

Until man is righteous, and *knows* that he is righteous, Satan reigns over him.

> For if by one man's offence death reigned by one; much more they which receive abundance of grace and of the gift of righteousness shall reign in life by one, Jesus Christ.
>
> Romans 5:17

We must be informed from God's Word of what belongs to us, and learn to honor God by the way we live. God is not pleased when we disregard any of the great redemptive work of Jesus. He desires to bring us out of the realm of slavery and servitude, and into our rightful position in the kingdom of God.

We must know:

We are redeemed.

We are new creation beings.

We are delivered from Satan's power.

We are free of all our sins.

When we know these things, we will not be easily shaken.

The moment we accept Jesus as Savior, we receive God's nature and become the righteousness of God in Christ Jesus.

> For he hath made him to be sin for us, who knew no sin; that we might be made the righteousness of God in him.
> II Corinthians 5:21

Jesus became sin for us. As a result, we can stand in the presence of Almighty God free of sin. God no longer looks at us as sinners. He sees us as the righteousness of God in Christ Jesus.

A sense of unworthiness, however it may be produced in our lives, destroys faith, robs us of our peace of mind, and makes us ineffectual Christians. It is a work of Satan.

If we have a feeling of inferiority, we cannot reign in life. We are IN HIM. We have been bought with a price, with the precious blood of Jesus, and we no longer belong to ourselves. (I Corinthians 6:19-20)

All of our success is in Him. We cannot fail when we understand that we have been made righteous.

We have no room for thoughts and feelings of inferiority.

We must replace those feelings with the knowledge of who we are in Christ Jesus.

I once talked with a lady who called me long distance. Her husband had continually told her she would go to hell if she put on lipstick or cut her hair. The woman had severe emotional problems from the strain of this constant condemnation. She knew that she could never be *good enough* to go to heaven.

Her husband did not understand that we are made righteous by the atoning blood of Jesus. He thought that our outward appearance was a sign of being righteous, or unrighteous. He desperately needed someone to help him.

Many people who believe such things are sincere and dedicated Christians. They are bound by denominational doctrines and ideas, but they can be free of such bondage and torment.

Let us examine two aspects of righteousness: the Divine Side and the Practical Application.

The Divine Side:

God, through Jesus Christ, has redeemed us.

> Even the righteousness of God which is by faith of Jesus Christ unto all and upon all them that believe: for there is no difference:
>
> For all have sinned, and come short of the glory of God;

> Being justified freely by his grace through the
> redemption that is in Christ Jesus.
>
> Romans 3:22-24

Our righteousness comes only by faith in Christ Jesus. We
have all sinned, but when we stand at the foot of the Cross,
we stand on level ground. We observe the Cross and em-
brace it with the knowledge that we have sinned, and
because of our faith in what He has done, we are forgiven.

Righteousness comes to us as a free gift. We can never
earn it. We will never be *good enough* to receive it. It does
not come by external observances—by keeping the law,
or wearing the proper clothing—it comes to us by faith
in Jesus Christ.

In the beginning, man was created to be a king who was
subject only to his Creator, but:

Man transgressed.

He was disloyal to God.

Man believed Satan.

He believed the devil's lie instead of
the Word of God.

Man lost dominion over his own kingdom.

Satan became the ruler of this world and the
prince of the power of the air.

Satan took over the entire kingdom that God
had commissioned to Adam.

Instead of living like a king, man became
a slave.

He became a slave to sin and Satan.

The Practical Application:

Every man alive must choose to live like a king, or he will automatically exist as a slave.

We have the power of choice to change our destiny! We should choose a personal relationship with Jesus. If we choose to live by rules and outward appearances, we are not going to live like kings.

In his letter to the Romans, Paul tells us that the Gospel is for the salvation of all men. (Romans 1:16) God has given to EVERY man the same measure of faith to believe on the Lord Jesus Christ. (Romans 12:3)

> But the righteousness which is of faith speaketh on this wise, Say not in thine heart, Who shall ascend into heaven? (that is, to bring Christ down from above:)
>
> Or, Who shall descend into the deep? (that is, to bring up Christ again from the dead.)
>
> But what saith it? The word is nigh thee, even in thy mouth, and in thy heart: that is, the word of faith, which we preach;
>
> That if thou shalt confess with thy mouth the Lord Jesus, and shalt believe in thine heart that God hath raised him from the dead, thou shalt be saved.
>
> For with the heart man believeth unto

righteousness; and with the mouth confession
is made unto salvation.
                                    Romans 10:6-10

This is the practical application to righteousness. The
righteousness which is of faith SPEAKETH! I want you
to say:

I AM RIGHTEOUS!

We are able to come before the Father and worship Him
because of what Jesus has done for us. We do not come
in our own righteousness, or our own goodness. We could
never be good enough even to please ourselves. We come
because we are the righteousness of God in Christ Jesus
by faith.

The Divine Side:

God, through Jesus Christ, has made us new creation
beings.

> Therefore if any man be in Christ, he is a new
> creature: old things are passed away; behold, all
> things are become new.
>   II Corinthians 5:17

> For he hath made him to be sin for us, who knew
> no sin; that we might be made the righteousness
> of God in him.
>   II Corinthians 5:21

God said, "Let us make man in our image, after our
likeness . . . " (Genesis 1:26) Man was created to show forth
the likeness of God.

When Jesus came to the earth as a man, He demonstrated to us the outward appearance of God. He also demonstrated to us the inward spiritual and moral nature of God. Jesus was God in a human body.

When Adam disobeyed God, the inner man died, but the outer man continued to live.

There are two families that dwell on the earth today—the family of God and the family of the devil. We are either children of God or children of the devil.

> Ye are of your father the devil, and the lusts of your father ye will do. He was a murderer from the beginning, and abode not in the truth, because there is no truth in him. When he speaketh a lie, he speaketh of his own: for he is a liar, and the father of it.
>
> John 8:44

> But he that is joined unto the Lord is one spirit.
>
> I Corinthians 6:17

The Practical Application:

Every man must choose to let the inner man dominate his life.

If we are going to live like kings, our spirits must be in control. Given a choice to love or to hate, our spirits will choose love. Given a choice to be encouraged or to be discouraged, we will choose to be encouraged. These decisions come out of the newly created spirit—the inner man. You can strengthen the inner man as you study the Word of God and begin to see what God says about you.

There is a story about a great, roaring lion and a little puppy. No one would ask, "Which one do you think can whip the other one?" What a foolish question!

You could change the outcome of that fight, however. All you would need to do is stop feeding the lion and start feeding the puppy. If you were patient and continually fed that puppy week after week, he would become strong and healthy. After a time, the lion would become so weak that he could no longer lift his paw.

When you become a Christian, your inner nature is like that little puppy. It must be fed, taught, and trained. Your outer, fleshly nature, like the lion, must be starved until it has no strength.

The people who live without victory are those who feed the lion. They spend very little time in Bible study. They are unconcerned about attending a good Bible teaching church. They sit in front of television sets and feed their carnal natures by the hour. The old lion roars and they wonder why they do not walk in victory.

What you feed your spirit is very important. The new inner spirit will not grow as you eat a steak. It must have spiritual food.

> It is the spirit that quickeneth; the flesh profiteth nothing: the words that I speak unto you,

they are spirit, and they are life.

John 6:63

The devil's trick is to keep us in doctrinal chains and hide the great truths of God from us. For years I was kept in ignorance.

As a minister, I walked in all the light I knew. I am sure other denominational ministers are doing all they know to do also, but many of us were kept in ignorance. We trusted our teachers, and were not taught the complete truths of God's Word.

We were taught fear and condemnation. We were beaten down and constantly reminded of how weak and unworthy we were.

It was my joy as a preacher to nail people's hides to the wall. I really let them know how bad they were. The more I did it, the more they bragged on me. They thought that was good preaching.

There was a little bird who was hatched in a cage. He did not know anything about life outside of that cage. He had never been outside. As he grew, he began to notice those things on his sides. He wondered what they were.

One day he learned that his wings would lift up and down. He flapped his wings so fast that he flew into the side of the cage. He did that over and over. Deep inside he heard a little voice saying, "You are not made for a cage." But that was the only home he knew.

Then, someone opened the door of the cage and the bird flew out for the first time. Can't you hear that little bird saying, "This is it! I was made for something bigger than a cage!"

The devil has made certain that the Body of Christ is all caged up. We have been fed bird seed when we were made to be eagles.

Millions of Christians are behind cages, locked up in doctrines that say miracles have passed away and the days of supernatural direction are over.

By the power of the Holy Spirit, these denominational cages are being opened and we are beginning to fly together. We are learning the great truths of the Word of God. We are experiencing the victorious life of Jesus Christ!

The Divine Side:

God, through Jesus Christ, has delivered us from Satan's power.

> Giving thanks unto the Father, which hath made us meet to be partakers of the inheritance of the saints in light:
>
> Who hath delivered us from the power of darkness, and hath translated us into the kingdom of his dear Son.
>
> Colossians 1:12-13

God has delivered us from the authority of Satan. It is not something we need to ask God to do for us. HE HAS ALREADY DONE IT! It is an eternal truth!

> Beware lest any man spoil you through philosophy and vain deceit, after the tradition of men, after the rudiments of the world, and not after Christ.
>
> And ye are complete in him, which is the head of all principality and power.
>
> And having spoiled principalities and powers, he made a shew of them openly, triumphing over them in it.
> Colossians 2:8,10,15

Many times we try to win the battles of life with philosophy or the traditions of men.

Jesus has spoiled principalities and powers, and if we will bind those forces in our daily prayer lives, we will see the manifestation of the things for which we are believing God.

The Practical Application:

Every Christian must study the Word of God and learn to defeat his enemy, the devil, for himself.

The way to do this is through prayer. We must say what the Word of God says. We must learn to pray in the Holy Spirit until we see the desired results.

> Put on the whole armour of God, that ye may

be able to stand against the wiles of the devil.

RESIST THE DEVIL!

For we wrestle not against flesh and blood, but against principalities, against powers, against the rulers of the darkness of this world, against spiritual wickedness in high places.

KNOW YOUR ENEMY!

Wherefore take unto you the whole armour of God, that ye may be able to withstand in the evil day, and having done all, to stand.

RESIST TEMPTATION!

Stand therefore, having your loins girt about with truth, and having on the breastplate of righteousness;

KNOW WHO YOU ARE IN CHRIST!

And your feet shod with the preparation of the gospel of peace;

BE PEACEFUL!

Above all, taking the shield of faith, wherewith ye shall be able to quench all the fiery darts of the wicked.

DO NOT GIVE UP!

And take the helmet of salvation, and the sword of the Spirit, which is the word of God:

SPEAK THE WORD!

> Praying always with all prayer and supplication
> in the Spirit, and watching thereunto with all
> perseverance and supplication for all saints.
>
> PRAY ALWAYS!
>
> Ephesians 6:11-18

God wants us to rule and reign over the devil in this life through PRAYER!

The Divine Side:

God, through Jesus Christ, has forgiven all our sins.

> In whom we have redemption through his blood,
> the forgiveness of sins, according to the riches
> of his grace.
>
> Ephesians 1:7

Our sins are forgiven, not on the basis of the sins we have committed, but on the basis of the riches of His grace. God's grace is rich and free!

Have you ever held a tiny baby? You admire that baby and talk about how sweet it is. That baby has no past. As a newborn Christian, you have no past.

I do not care what your past was. I do not care how many crimes you have committed. When you come to God, your past ceases to exist.

The Practical Application:

Every believer of the Lord Jesus Christ must learn to act on the Word of God instead of on what he sees, feels, or hears.

When it seems that you have failed, do not condemn yourself.

> There is therefore now no condemnation to them which are in Christ Jesus, who walk not after the flesh, but after the Spirit.
>
> Romans 8:1

If you feel that you have missed God or failed your fellowman, do not continue in that state of mind!

> But if we walk in the light, as he is in the light, we have fellowship one with another, and the blood of Jesus Christ his Son cleanseth us from all sin.
>
> If we confess our sins, he is faithful and just to forgive us our sins, and to cleanse us from all unrighteousness.
>
> I John 1:7,9

Be quick to get back into the light. Confess your sin and believe that He has cleansed you.

> Let the redeemed of the Lord say so, whom he hath redeemed from the hand of the enemy.
>
> Psalm 107:2

The secret of victory is acting fearlessly and confessing boldly! Satan is afraid of you!

> God, through Jesus Christ, has redeemed you.
>
> God, through Jesus Christ, has made you a new creature.
>
> God, through Jesus Christ, has delivered you from Satan's power.
>
> God, through Jesus Christ, has forgiven all your sins.

WE REIGN IN LIFE AS KINGS
THROUGH THE GIFT OF RIGHTEOUSNESS.

Five

Reigning in Life Through the Name of Jesus

We can reign in life as kings through the wonderful Name of Jesus.

> Let the word of Christ dwell in you richly in all wisdom; teaching and admonishing one another in psalms and hymns and spiritual songs, singing with grace in your hearts to the Lord.
>
> And whatsoever ye do in word or deed, do all in the name of the Lord Jesus, giving thanks to God and the Father by him.
>
> Colossians 3:16-17

In order to reign in life, we must understand that we do everything in the Name of the Lord Jesus Christ.

We do not have to tolerate what the devil throws at us. We do not have to worm our way through life, crying and putting up with all his evil schemes. We allow the devil to have freedom in our lives because of ignorance or inactivity.

God created us to live an abundant life. We will begin to partake of that abundance as we learn to exercise authority in the Name of Jesus.

> The Name of Jesus means much to the Father.
>
> That Name means much to the Body of Christ.
>
> His Name means much to the devil and demon forces.

Often, we gather under good names such as Baptist, Methodist, or Church of God, but we have almost ignored the Name of Jesus. Today the denominational names are growing dimmer and the Name of Jesus is growing brighter!

At the right hand of God, Jesus holds the highest position in the universe.

> Which he wrought in Christ, when he raised him from the dead, and set him at his own right hand in the heavenly places,
>
> Far above all principality, and power, and might, and dominion, and every name that is named, not only in this world, but also in that which is to come.
>
> Ephesians 1:20-21

Because of His position, Jesus owns everything. He is the heir of all things.

> God, who at sundry times and in divers manners spake in time past unto the fathers by the prophets,

> Hath in these last days spoken unto us by his
> Son, whom he hath appointed heir of all things,
> by whom also he made the worlds.
>
> Hebrews 1:1-2

**Because of His position, the Name of Jesus holds the
highest authority in the spirit realm.**

No matter what your struggle may be, it is with spirit beings without bodies. Our battle is not with people, but with
the rulers of the darkness of this world. (Ephesians 6:12)
Jesus is the Name that holds all authority in the area
where those spirit beings live, and God requires us to use
that Name.

THE NAME OF JESUS IS THE MOST POWERFUL NAME IN THE UNIVERSE!

> Let this mind be in you, which was also in Christ
> Jesus:
>
> Who, being in the form of God, thought it not
> robbery to be equal with God:
>
> But made himself of no reputation, and took
> upon him the form of a servant, and was made
> in the likeness of men:
>
> And being found in fashion as a man, he hum-
> bled himself, and became obedient unto death,
> even the death of the cross.
>
> Wherefore God also hath highly exalted him,
> and given him a name which is above every
> name:

> That at the name of Jesus every knee should
> bow, of things in heaven, and things in earth,
> and things under the earth;
>
> And that every tongue should confess that
> Jesus Christ is Lord, to the glory of God the
> Father.
>
> Philippians 2:5-11

Jesus gave us the right to use His name.

Recently, an attorney who represents me in another city,
called my office. In the conversation, he said that he was
sending me a form to sign, a power of attorney. He needed legal permission to use my name. It was necessary for
him to take action on my behalf in a location where it was
not possible for me to be. By signing this form, I gave him
the right to act in my behalf.

That is exactly what Jesus did when He gave us the right
to use His Name.

> Verily, verily, I say unto you, He that believeth
> on me, the works that I do shall he do also; and
> greater works than these shall he do; because
> I go unto my Father.
>
> And whatsoever ye shall ask in my name, that
> will I do, that the Father may be glorified in the
> Son.
>
> If ye shall ask any thing in my name, I will do it.
>
> John 14:12-14

We should do the works that Jesus did. Think about all
the blind people, the deaf people, and the demon pos-

sessed people whom Jesus healed. He said, "The works that I do, you can do."

Jesus said we can ask anything in His Name. The word *ask* in the Greek actually means *demand*. However, we should never demand things from God in an arrogant manner.

Instead, we should search the Word of God and come boldly to Him, saying, "This is mine according to Your Word." When we do this, we will know that we are praying according to God's will. God will see to it that it is done. He will see that sickness, disease, and demon powers leave us.

> But the Comforter, which is the Holy Ghost, whom the Father will send in my name, he shall teach you all things, and bring all things to your remembrance, whatsoever I have said unto you.
>
> John 14:26

> Ye have not chosen me, but I have chosen you, and ordained you, that ye should go and bring forth fruit, and that your fruit should remain: that whatsoever ye shall ask of the Father in my name, he may give it you.
>
> John 15:16

We know that we do not pray to Jesus. The Bible says we should pray to the Father in the Name of Jesus.

> And in that day ye shall ask me nothing. Verily, verily, I say unto you, Whatsoever ye shall ask the Father in my name, he will give it you.

> Hitherto have ye asked nothing in my name:
> ask, and ye shall receive, that your joy may be
> full.
>
> John 16:23-24

Just before Jesus was received up into heaven, He appeared to the eleven disciples and gave them the Great Commission.

> And he said unto them, Go ye into all the world,
> and preach the gospel to every creature.
>
> He that believeth and is baptized shall be
> saved; but he that believeth not shall be
> damned.
>
> And these signs shall follow them that believe;
> In my name shall they cast out devils; they shall
> speak with new tongues;
>
> They shall take up serpents; and if they drink
> any deadly thing, it shall not hurt them; they
> shall lay hands on the sick, and they shall
> recover.
>
> Mark 16:15-18

The Holy Spirit is our Teacher. He will teach us how to use the Name of Jesus.

> Now we have received, not the spirit of the
> world, but the spirit which is of God; that we
> might know the things that are freely given to
> us of God.
>
> Which things also we speak, not in the words
> which man's wisdom teacheth, but which the
> Holy Ghost teacheth; comparing spiritual

things with spiritual.
                              I Corinthians 2:12-13

The Holy Spirit is in us to help us recognize the Lordship of Jesus and KNOW that the Name of Jesus is above every name. The Apostle Paul prayed that God would give the Ephesians a spirit of wisdom and revelation in the knowledge of HIM. (Ephesians 1:17)

The Holy Spirit dwells within each person who has confessed Jesus Christ as his or her Savior. He is ever present within us. Our bodies are the temples of the Holy Spirit and He is indeed our Teacher, if we allow Him to be. (I Corinthians 6:19-20)

Our oldest son, Paul, who is now a practicing physician, proved this as a young Oral Roberts University student.

The summer of his junior year, Paul went with a missions group to Africa. During this time, he became very ill with malaria. He had a very high fever, chills, and muscular spasms so severe that his teeth chattered. He was left alone for three days and was too sick to pray, or even to think.

While he was sick, the Word of God began to come up out of Paul's spirit and into his mind. He began to think on the Name of Jesus—the Name that is above every sickness and disease. He was still too sick to speak, but the Holy Spirit brought to Paul's memory healing scriptures that he had memorized in the past.

The Holy Spirit does not get sick, and He was inside Paul!

The fever broke, the chills dissipated, and his body became normal.

The Book of Acts is a record of how the New Testament believers shook the heathen world by using the Name of Jesus. The Gospel did not revolve around a man, an organization, or a denomination.

The believers preached salvation in the Name of Jesus.

> And it shall come to pass, that whosoever shall call on the name of the Lord shall be saved.
>
> Acts 2:21

New believers were baptized in the Name of Jesus.

> Then Peter said unto them, Repent, and be baptized every one of you in the name of Jesus Christ for the remission of sins, and ye shall receive the gift of the Holy Ghost.
>
> Acts 2:38

The believers brought physical healing to many through the Name of Jesus.

Jesus had been put to death by the religious and political leaders. After His death, burial, and resurrection, the believers had gathered in the upper room and received the infilling of the Holy Spirit.

Very soon after this experience, Peter and John went up together into the temple. They saw a man who was lame from his mother's womb, and he asked Peter and John for alms.

> Then Peter said, Silver and gold have I none;
> but such as I have give I thee: In the name of
> Jesus Christ of Nazareth rise up and walk.
>
> Acts 3:6

The same people who were responsible for the death of Jesus must have been in the city when this crippled man received his healing. They recognized that this man was now walking and leaping and praising God. Peter was quick to tell the people that it was not his power or holiness that made this man strong. He was healed through the Name of Jesus.

> And his name through faith in his name hath
> made this man strong, whom ye see and know:
> yea, the faith which is by him hath given him
> this perfect soundness in the presence of you all.
>
> Acts 3:16

The believers suffered persecution because of the Name of Jesus.

The religious and political leaders recognized the power in the Name of Jesus. They became so angry that they took Peter and John to trial.

> Then Peter, filled with the Holy Ghost, said un-
> to them, Ye rulers of the people, and elders of
> Israel,
>
> If we this day be examined of the good deed

done to the impotent man, by what means he is made whole;

Be it known unto you all, and to all the people of Israel, that by the name of Jesus Christ of Nazareth, whom ye crucified, whom God raised from the dead, even by him doth this man stand here before you whole.

This is the stone which was set at nought of you builders, which is become the head of the corner.

Neither is there salvation in any other: for there is none other name under heaven given among men, whereby we must be saved.

Now when they saw the boldness of Peter and John, and perceived that they were unlearned and ignorant men, they marvelled; and they took knowledge of them, that they had been with Jesus.

And beholding the man which was healed standing with them, they could say nothing against it.

But when they had commanded them to go aside out of the council, they conferred among themselves,

Saying, What shall we do to these men? for that indeed a notable miracle hath been done by them is manifest to all them that dwell in Jerusalem; and we cannot deny it.

But that it spread no further among the people, let us straitly threaten them, that they speak henceforth to no man in this name.

> And they called them, and commanded them
> not to speak at all nor teach in the name of
> Jesus.
>
> Acts 4:8-18

The high priest, the captain of the temple, and the chief
priests gathered, not against a political party or an army,
but against the NAME OF JESUS.

Peter and John were threatened and released, but notice
their boldness.

> And now, Lord, behold their threatenings: and
> grant unto thy servants, that with all boldness
> they may speak thy word,
>
> By stretching forth thine hand to heal; and that
> signs and wonders may be done by the name of
> thy holy child Jesus.
>
> Acts 4:29-30

When the disciples prayed that way, the place was shaken
and all who were assembled together were filled with the
Holy Ghost. Again they were put in jail, but an angel let
them out! Finally, they were taken before the Sanhedrin.

> And when they had brought them, they set
> them before the council: and the high priest
> asked them,
>
> Saying, Did not we straitly command you that
> ye should not teach in this name? and, behold,
> ye have filled Jerusalem with your doctrine, and
> intend to bring this man's blood upon us.
>
> Acts 5:27-28

> . . . and when they had called the apostles, and
> beaten them, they commanded that they should
> not speak in the name of Jesus, and let them go.
>
> And they departed from the presence of the
> council, rejoicing that they were counted wor-
> thy to suffer shame for his name.
>
> And daily in the temple, and in every house,
> they ceased not to teach and preach Jesus
> Christ.
>
> Acts 5:40b-42

The believers counted it a joy to suffer for the Name of
Jesus.

Often, Christians are persecuted for believing that God's
Word is true. It is easy for us to be discouraged when we
suffer persecution, but the New Testament Christians considered it a joyful experience. They asked for more
boldness!

The disciples counted it an honor to suffer for the Name
of Jesus.

In the Book of Acts, the Name of Jesus stirred the world,
broke Satan's power, healed the sick, and wrought
miracles. It will do the same today!

In the early church, that Name, spoken by believers who
were filled with the Holy Spirit, wrought the same miracles
that Jesus did while He was on earth.

> For where two or three are gathered together

> in my name, there am I in the midst of them.
>
> Matthew 18:20

When we use His Name, it is as if Jesus Himself were speaking through our lips.

The Name of Jesus, used by believers, has power to do what Jesus did and even more.

The youngest of believers, filled with the Holy Ghost, can speak that Name in faith to perform miracles. It will work for us just as it did for Jesus when He spoke in the Name of the Father.

It does not matter how unlearned you may be or what people may think of you, the Name of Jesus used against Satan has all the power you will ever need.

A minister friend of mine related this story to me as it happened to him. One afternoon, as he was resting, my friend experienced his spirit leaving his body.

He told me that suddenly he found himself in a dark, misty atmosphere, and he was afraid. He did not know where he was, and he had a terrible awareness of being lost. He sensed the presence of something approaching him. Terrified, he recognized Satan.

Instantly, Jesus appeared between my friend and Satan. Jesus faced the devil with His back to my friend. He said that Jesus, very slowly and gently, began to step backwards toward him until the face of Jesus became the face of my friend, the torso of Jesus became his torso, the

legs of Jesus became his legs, the feet of Jesus became
his feet, the arms of Jesus became his arms, the fingers
of Jesus became his fingers.

Jesus, in my friend, raised his arm and pointed his finger
directly at Satan, and he heard himself say, "Satan, you
shall bow!" Satan fell to the ground!

Jesus lives in each one of us. Our faces are like His face.
Our hands are like His hands. When we speak, He speaks!
Satan must bow to the Name of Jesus.

WE REIGN IN LIFE AS KINGS
THROUGH THE NAME OF JESUS.

Six

Reigning in Life Through the Confession of God's Word

You can reign in life by your continual confession of God's Word.

In the nineteenth chapter of the Book of Acts, Paul arrived in Ephesus and found twelve disciples of John the Baptist. They were twelve believers without the power of the Holy Ghost.

> He said unto them, Have ye received the Holy Ghost since ye believed? And they said unto him, We have not so much as heard whether there be any Holy Ghost.
>
> And he said unto them, Unto what then were ye baptized? And they said, Unto John's baptism.
>
> And when Paul had laid his hands upon them, the Holy Ghost came on them; and they spake with tongues, and prophesied.
>
> Acts 19:2,3,6

These twelve disciples received the Holy Ghost and there was a great revival. They stirred up the synagogue so much that they were kicked out. They moved on, and for two years the revival continued as the Word of God was preached.

> Many of them also which used curious arts brought their books together, and burned them before all men: and they counted the price of them, and found it fifty thousand pieces of silver.
>
> So mightily grew the word of God and prevailed.
>
> Acts 19:19-20

The Word of God prevailed. *Prevail* means to triumph or win a victory; to be greater in strength or influence. The Word of God grew so mightily that it triumphed! The Word of God overcame and conquered!

We must learn to confess God's Word until it is a prevailing power in our lives.

Many people hear a message on confession and immediately say, "I confess I am going to have a new Cadillac." When they do not receive the Cadillac, they declare that there is nothing to confessing the Word of God. The problem was that they were not confessing God's Word.

The Bible says the Word of God grew so mightily that it prevailed. It conquered! When you allow the Word of God to grow in you, believe it in your heart, and continually confess it with your mouth, it will prevail in your life!

It may not occur the first time you say it, but if you will believe what God says, the Word of God will prevail over every sickness, every disease, every fear, every torment, and every situation you may have in your life. Your responsibility is to learn to confess the Word of God until it prevails.

Many times I have started a confession in weakness. I have had a lack of understanding and belief, but as I remained faithful to that confession, the Word of God has prevailed.

Several years ago I injured my back. At times, as I was driving my car, a stream of fire would go down my leg and the pain would be so great I had to pull over to the side of the road and get out, and walk around. The pain in my leg was great, but the Word of God said I was healed.

I began to declare that God had healed my body. I did not feel healed. One Sunday morning as I stood up to preach, I was in such pain that I had to hold on to the pulpit. I made my confession to the congregation, "I am so happy. The Lord has completely healed my back!" The people became excited and began to rejoice in the Lord. I rejoiced with them and the healing of my back was manifested soon after that morning.

> And Jesus answering saith unto them, Have faith in God.
>
> For verily I say unto you, That whosoever shall say unto this mountain, Be thou removed, and be thou cast into the sea; and shall not doubt

> in his heart, but shall believe that those things
> which he saith shall come to pass; he shall have
> whatsoever he saith.
>
> Mark 11:22-23

You are ruled in life by your confessions. You may say
that you do not believe in confession, and that it does not
make any difference what you say or what you believe,
but confession is working for you anyway.

> Death and life are in the power of the tongue:
> and they that love it shall eat the fruit thereof.
>
> Proverbs 18:21

It is a law of God. That law is in operation whether you
believe in it or not. Therefore, you should allow it to work
good in your life rather than evil. If you learn to confess
what God says about you rather than what you see and
hear, the Word of God will prevail!

Suppose you are afflicted with a weakness in your heart,
and you begin to confess you are healed. You do not talk
about the doctor's report, or about how long you may have
to live. You do not confess all the things you cannot do
because of that weak heart.

Instead your statements are, "God's Word says that by
His stripes I am healed. My confession lines up with His
Word. By the stripes of Jesus, my heart is healed. I rebuke
fear in the Name of Jesus! I will not believe a lie of the
devil!"

As you continue to confess God's Word in your conversation and in your mind, the day will come when the attack of Satan will have no effect on you because the issue was settled by the Word of God in your spirit.

Your spirit may not become strong overnight. The devil will contest every step you take.

The Word of God must grow in our hearts until it prevails, rules, and reigns over every doubt, every symptom, and every trouble that is aligned against us.

We are spoiled in America. We want instant potatoes, instant coffee, instant everything. We also want instant healing. It is wonderful to receive an instant solution for the problem we face. However, if it does not come instantly, we must stay with God's Word until that Word prevails in our lives.

We cannot drive the enemy away by sitting and gazing at the television. I own several television sets, but I do not change the situations in my life by sitting in front of them. The changes in my life cannot be produced there.

If there was ever a day in human history when we need to be hiding the Word of God in our hearts, this is the day! The conditions of Sodom and Gomorrah are developing around us. We should be sanctified people, set apart for God by His Word. We need to hear from God.

We must learn to look at God's Word and meditate on the scriptures until they become a part of us. We need to sit down with our Bibles, quietly meditate on God's Word, and allow God to speak to us. That is a visit with the Master. He will speak to our hearts and communicate with us through His Word.

It took me a long time to learn this. I thought my relationship with God was based on how much scripture I read and how many facts I knew.

We should read the Bible until we know it inside and out, but we must also learn to meditate upon God's Word until it becomes a part of us. God will then speak to our spirits and communicate with us through His Word.

I have thought about a verse of scripture and spoken in tongues over it until that particular passage became clear to my understanding. I was aglow with communication from God. That section of the Bible has now become a part of my spirit and nothing can shake that truth from me. I know when the great Creator has spoken a word to my heart.

God is a Spirit. God spoke in the beginning and said, "Let there be . . .", and He created the whole universe with words. When a spirit speaks, there is creative power.

I am a spirit. You are a spirit. Many times we do not speak from our spirits, but from our minds. If we allow the Word of God to become strong in our spirits, the words we speak will come from our spirits. They will be creative words.

There will come a day when you will say out of your spirit, "I know I am healed!" You will not have to pray about it anymore.

I want you to say:

> GOD IS A SPIRIT.

> I AM A SPIRIT.

We must take time to learn to speak God's Word. We have that Word recorded in the Bible.

We do not place the Word of God into our spirits overnight. We must hold fast to our confession until the Word of God reigns in our spirits. Then we will reign in life as kings.

We have not only been made kings, but we have been made PRIESTS.

> And hath made us kings and priests unto God and his Father; to him be glory and dominion for ever and ever. Amen.
>
> Revelation 1:6

Jesus is our great HIGH PRIEST.

> Seeing then that we have a great high priest, that is passed into the heavens, Jesus the Son of God, let us hold fast our profession (confession).
>
> For we have not an high priest which cannot be touched with the feeling of our infirmities; but was in all points tempted like as we are, yet without sin.
>
> Let us therefore come boldly unto the throne of grace, that we may obtain mercy, and find grace

to help in time of need.

                                                    Hebrews 4:14-16

Jesus is indeed our great High Priest. He is our High Priest NOW. He has passed through the heavens and is seated at the right hand of our Father, waiting for our confession. When we confess the Word of God, Jesus, as our High Priest, will take it before the Father.

Jesus represents us before God. He is touched with our feelings and weaknesses. He knows every problem that we face as human beings. He understands, and He desires that we come boldly to His throne of grace. He wants to help us when we have a need.

Jesus was tempted in all areas as we are today. We tend to think of this passage of scripture as it relates to our failures and our weaknesses, but it has another meaning. Jesus suffered being tempted, nevertheless, He chose to obey the Father and fulfill God's plan for His life.

Jesus is our High Priest not only in times of weakness, but in our times of total commitment to what God has shown us to do. Many times it is at this point in our lives when Jesus becomes the most precious to us. Jesus, as our High Priest, brings us to God and into fellowship with our Heavenly Father.

There may be times when we feel utter despair; Jesus has been there, too. He is there with us NOW. We must hold fast to our confessions!

Jesus is our faithful High Priest, and He will take our

words before the Father.

In order to reign in life we, too, must learn to minister as a priest by continually confessing the Word of God. As we confess the Word of God, we show forth His praise.

> But ye are a chosen generation, a royal priesthood, an holy nation, a peculiar people; that ye should shew forth the praises of him who hath called you out of darkness into his marvellous light.
>
> I Peter 2:9

I had a friend who was a great pianist. Years before, he had been offered a position with a Hollywood personality, but he chose to do the work of the Lord. He became afflicted with arthritis. His knees became as big as grapefruits. His arms and wrists were knotted up, and his body was bent over. He could no longer play the piano.

Many people prayed for him. He studied the Word of God, and acted as a priest by continually confessing God's Word.

After months of seeking God and holding fast to his confession, he was flying in an airplane to preach in another city. He was meditating on the Word of God and quietly praising God that His Word was true, and suddenly, the scripture verse, "By His stripes ye were healed," went from his mind into his spirit. He spoke out boldly, "I AM HEALED!"

He walked off the airplane and his body was still twisted.

The person that picked him up at the airport asked how he was and he declared that he was healed. That night, as he stood in the pulpit for the evening service, he said, "Thank God I am healed!"

The Word of God had gotten down into his spirit and he KNEW he was healed.

> By him therefore let us offer the sacrifice of praise to God continually, that is, the fruit of our lips giving thanks to his name.
>
> Hebrews 13:15

He held fast to his confession until the Word of God traveled from his mind to his spirit. He no longer asked for healing, he thanked God that it was already done. After the experience on the plane, he began to improve. The Word of God grew so mightily that it prevailed over his physical condition. Today he is enjoying a normal physical body!

If we want to reign in life, we must learn to speak the Word of God. We must give Jesus, our High Priest, something with which to work. We cannot speak like a beggar and live like a king.

Make this confession:

I AM A KING!

We must confess the Word of God until it prevails over our normal thinking processes. It must be confessed until it prevails over our natural five senses. When Jesus confessed, "My Father is greater than all," He knew exactly what He was doing. He was holding fast to His confession.

How do you speak to God? What is your confession? I want you to say:

MY FATHER IS GREATER THAN ALL!

As young children, we talked as if our daddy could whip any other daddy alive. If our fathers had known how we boasted of their great strength, it would have worried them! That is the way we should speak of our Heavenly Father.

We should say, "My Father can whip your father!" We could even say, "My Father has already whipped you, devil, and I can whip you in the Name of Jesus!" We must not limit God. He is a big God. All things are possible with Him. (Mark 10:27)

Jesus continually confessed:

"My Father is greater than all."

"My Father and I are one."

"My Father loves me."

"The Father, in me, doeth the works."

"He that has seen me has seen the Father."

This Word in Jesus prevailed over the laws of nature. It was contrary to natural human thinking.

The Word of God prevailed over Abraham's natural senses when he looked at his body. God promised him that he and Sarah would have a son. Abraham considered not his own body, but believed God. (Romans 4:17-22)

Boldness is necessary in a healthy Christian life. We must come boldly to the throne of grace in order to obtain mercy and find the help we need!

The life story of Lillian B. Yeomans is beautiful. She was a physician who had become addicted to drugs. She was dying, but God healed her and completely delivered her from drug addiction. She was so touched by God that she left her medical practice and followed the Lord into a ministry of healing.

She developed a home where she could nurse dying, hopeless people. She taught them the Word of God. One day a lady, who was in the last stage of tuberculosis, arrived for help. Dr. Yeomans read to the woman from the twenty-eighth chapter of Deuteronomy about the curse of the law.

> The Lord shall smite thee with a consumption, and with a fever, and with an inflammation, and with an extreme burning, and with the sword, and with blasting, and with mildew; and they shall pursue thee until thou perish.
>
> Deuteronomy 28:22

The lady understood that consumption was a curse of the law. Then, Dr. Yeomans read another verse of scripture to her.

> Christ hath redeemed us from the curse of the

law, being made a curse for us: for it is written, Cursed is every one that hangeth on a tree.

Galatians 3:13

She learned that she was redeemed from the curse of the law through Jesus Christ. Dr. Yeomans gave her a prescription. The woman was to say over and over every day:

> According to Deuteronomy 28:22, this consumption is a curse of the law.
>
> According to Galatians 3:13, Christ has redeemed me from the curse of the law.
>
> Therefore, I do not have consumption in my body.

The woman followed these instructions for days, confessing the Word of God.

Finally, the lady said, "This is not doing any good. I am making no progress. It is just a bunch of words, and I am like a parrot going on and on with no results."

The doctor insisted she continue.

Days later, the woman burst into the kitchen, saying, "Dr. Yeomans, did you know that according to Deuteronomy 28:22, consumption is a curse of the law? Did you know that I am redeemed from the curse of the law? Christ has redeemed me from the curse of the law!" She began to get better from that day until she was completely healed.

Let the Word of God prevail in you until you see that God

has told you the truth. Act as a priest, knowing that Jesus is your High Priest. One day that Word will drop from your head into your spirit, creating the perfect answer for which you have been believing!

Do not spend your time saying what the devil has done or what he is doing. Instead say what you have in Christ. Confess what you can do through Christ. Talk about what God has done and is doing for you. Say it boldly!

There are four steps you can take that will help you to reign in life.

Step One: Confess the Word of God and the promises of God until they become a reality in your spirit. Do not get discouraged.

Step Two: Make your plans as though the promise in which you are believing for has already manifested itself.

Step Three: Keep the visual image of its reality before you.

Step Four: Continually rejoice from your heart as you would at the very moment the promise is actually manifested.

I have the following ten facts written in the back of my Bible in green ink. I boldly confess them.

> I am a new creature in Christ Jesus.
>
> I am the righteousness of God in Christ Jesus.
>
> I am more than a conqueror.

I am strong in the Lord and in the power of His might.

I am healed by the stripes of Jesus.

I am delivered from the power of darkness.

I am translated into the kingdom of His dear Son.

I am redeemed from the curse of the law.

I am a prosperous person because Jesus became poor that I might be rich.

We are priests. Jesus is our faithful High Priest.

WE REIGN IN LIFE AS KINGS BY OUR CONTINUAL CONFESSION OF GOD'S WORD.

Seven

Reigning in Life Through Forgiveness

One day I was talking to the Lord about healing. I was thinking of the healings Jesus had performed while He was on earth. I said, "Lord, I know You must have been a great healing preacher. I wish I could have been there to hear some of Your healing sermons."

The Lord said to me, "You have them in the Bible. Read Matthew, Mark, Luke, and John. That is what I taught. If the people believed and acted on it, then they were healed. If they listened to Me and refused to believe what I taught, then I could not heal them even though I was there in person."

I realized that in the Gospels, I had the healing sermons of Jesus. I am sure those are not all of His sermons, but they are the ones that God felt we needed.

When I teach what Jesus taught in the Bible, people receive lasting healings and miracles from God. The truths that Jesus taught in the Bible usually do not make people run and jump with joy. They are serious subjects that have to be dealt with in every area of life.

Jesus had much to say about forgiveness.

> Moreover if thy brother shall trespass against thee, go and tell him his fault between thee and him alone: if he shall hear thee, thou hast gained thy brother.
>
> But if he will not hear thee, then take with thee one or two more, that in the mouth of two or three witnesses every word may be established.
>
> Matthew 18:15-16

It is not strange that Jesus would preach about brothers having fights and disagreements. Jesus' teachings got down to the real nitty-gritty of life.

Peter could not get the idea of forgiveness out of his mind.

> Then came Peter to him, and said, Lord, how oft shall my brother sin against me, and I forgive him? till seven times?
>
> Jesus saith unto him, I say not unto thee, Until seven times: but, Until seventy times seven.
>
> Matthew 18:21-22

Jesus said we are to forgive our brother or sister four hundred and ninety times! In other words, forgiveness is an attitude; it is a way of life.

I remember a fellow who transgressed against me. He

treated me so badly that I felt like choking him! After he had wronged me, I wrote him a real nasty letter, but I tore it up. I had to forgive him. Jesus gave me no other choice.

When we learn to forgive others as God has forgiven us, we will reign in life as kings over every heartache, hurt, and situation.

Jesus continued His sermon, explaining the importance of forgiveness.

> Therefore is the kingdom of heaven likened unto a certain king, which would take account of his servants.
>
> And when he had begun to reckon, one was brought unto him, which owed him ten thousand talents.
>
> But forasmuch as he had not to pay, his lord commanded him to be sold, and his wife, and children, and all that he had, and payment to be made.
>
> The servant therefore fell down, and worshipped him, saying, Lord, have patience with me, and I will pay thee all.
>
> Then the lord of that servant was moved with compassion, and loosed him, and forgave him the debt.
>
> But that same servant went out, and found one of his fellow-servants, which owed him an hundred pence: and he laid hands on him, and took him by the throat, saying, Pay me that thou owest.

And his fellow-servant fell down at his feet, and besought him, saying, Have patience with me, and I will pay thee all.

And he would not: but went and cast him into prison, till he should pay the debt.

So when his fellow-servants saw what was done, they were very sorry, and came and told unto their lord all that was done.

Then his lord, after that he had called him, said unto him, O thou wicked servant, I forgave thee all that debt, because thou desiredst me:

Shouldest not thou also have had compassion on thy fellow-servant, even as I had pity on thee?

And his lord was wroth, and delivered him to the tormentors, till he should pay all that was due unto him.

So likewise shall my heavenly Father do also unto you, if ye from your hearts forgive not every one his brother their trespasses.

                                              Matthew 18:23-35

This is not my sermon, it is Jesus' sermon. This is not my doctrine, it is the doctrine of Jesus.

There are three very important facts about unforgiveness to be learned from this passage of scripture.

First, the master said that his servant was wicked because he did not forgive his fellowservant. God looks at our failure to forgive as wickedness. God forgave us from all the sins of our past, and He continues to forgive us when we fail even after we have been born again. How much more should we forgive others!

Second, the master was angry with the servant who did not forgive his fellowservant. Unforgiveness in our lives provokes the anger of God. If we are going to live a life that is pleasing to God, we must live a life of forgiveness.

Third, the master delivered his servant to the tormentors because he had failed to forgive. If we do not forgive, our Heavenly Father will have to deal with us in the same way we deal with others.

The place of torment is not hell. Thank God, Jesus paid the debt for us and we do not have to go to hell. If we continue to live in unforgiveness, the Bible says that God will deliver us over to the tormentors. We do not like to think about our Heavenly Father in this context. We do not like to think about discipline, but this servant was delivered to the tormentors until he could pay his debt. And Jesus, talking about His wonderful, righteous, loving, and merciful Father, said, "So likewise shall my heavenly Father do also unto you, if ye from your hearts forgive not every one his brother their trespasses."

That is not shouting ground; it is sober ground. That is the Head of the Church talking. Jesus is teaching us how to avoid being delivered to the tormentors.

Jesus said that a child of God can be delivered over to the

tormentors until he pays for his wrongdoings. He can be delivered to the tormentors until he forgives!

There is physical, mental, and spiritual torment. Physical torment is sickness and disease in our bodies. Mental torment produces confusion and fear. Spiritual torment is being accused by Satan. He is the accuser of the brethren. (Revelation 12:10)

I know a man who is a Methodist preacher. Every one of his fingers were bent over and twisted. He said, "Brother Osteen, one day I made a decision to start living a life of forgiveness."

Every time he thought of someone towards whom he had a wrong attitude, he would forgive them. He said, "I would lie in bed and think of people as I prayed. If someone came to my mind, I would forgive them. As I drove the car, if someone came to my mind, I would forgive them."

Several months after he made the decision to live in forgiveness, finger after finger straightened up, and healing came into his body. He is completely healed today!

> Therefore I say unto you, What things soever ye desire, when ye pray, believe that ye receive them, and ye shall have them.
>
> And when ye stand praying, forgive, if ye have aught against any: that your Father also which is in heaven may forgive you your trespasses.
>
> But if ye do not forgive, neither will your Father

which is in heaven forgive your trespasses.

                                             Mark 11:24-26

There was a woman in our church who had a large tumor.
We laid hands on her and prayed for her, but she did not
get healed. One service I taught on forgiveness. After-
wards this woman came to me and said, "I did not know
that unforgiveness was locked away within my heart. I
had no idea that I had anything against anyone."

She continued, "The Holy Spirit brought my mother-in-
law to my mind and something that happened years ago.
I was not aware that I held anything against her, but the
Holy Spirit showed me that I had resentment locked away
in the recesses of my heart. I had never truly forgiven her."

After she forgave her mother-in-law for something that
had happened years before, the tumor disappeared.

When you open yourself up to God and say, "God, search
my heart and show me how I can change!", then God will
help you.

FORGIVENESS and HEALING are closely related. Many
times people who are seeking healing really need to walk
in forgiveness.

Forgive and be healed! It may not always happen instantly, but it will happen!

Many divorced people have a battle with unforgiveness.
It is easy for a wife to have bitterness against a husband

who has mistreated her. It is easy for a husband to have resentment against a wife who has left him.

I have heard more than one wife say, "He is guilty. He ruined my life! He left me without anything to eat. I had to take care of the children by myself."

They are right; he is guilty. But, only the guilty need mercy. Guilty people must be forgiven, not for their sakes, but for ours! Why? Jesus tells us why in the following scriptures.

> For if ye forgive men their trespasses, your heavenly Father will also forgive you:
>
> But if ye forgive not men their trespasses, neither will your Father forgive your trespasses.
>
> Matthew 6:14-15

If you forgive, you WILL BE FORGIVEN. If you do not forgive, you WILL NOT BE FORGIVEN.

There is no alternative. God will only forgive us as we forgive others.

Jesus put the responsibility upon us. In the Lord's Prayer, Jesus again mentioned forgiveness.

> And forgive us our debts, as we forgive our debtors.
>
> Matthew 6:12

Resentment, bitterness, and unforgiveness release a

negative force within our entire beings. It is a very dangerous force that grows stronger each day we choose not to follow the teachings of Jesus.

The relationship between you and other members of your family is very important. The relationship between a mother-in-law and daughter-in-law is an area where there needs to be a searching of the heart; likewise, between father-in-law and son-in-law, between parents and children, and between brothers and sisters.

One day, as I allowed the Holy Spirit to search my heart, I found that I held things against my mother and daddy. They quarreled much, and I grew up resenting the tension that it produced. I lived in fear of them divorcing. I remember many times crying over their disputes.

As the Lord began to speak to me about the critical thoughts I had toward my parents, He reminded me that when I was a boy, my parents did not have an automatic washing machine. They did not have many of the conveniences that are plentiful in our day. We had a large family, and it had not been easy for my parents to raise us during the Great Depression. My heart was broken because of my wrong attitude.

I was a successful minister. God had blessed my life in many ways, yet I still had areas of unforgiveness in my heart.

Opening my heart to the Lord Jesus, I saw those unpleasant memories were actually areas of unforgiveness.

Parents have to be willing to forgive their children. Perhaps your children have really hurt you. They may be guilty of some terrible wrong, but you must forgive. As you forgive them, you will be forgiven, and healing will come to your spirit, mind, and body.

When you walk in forgiveness, you open the door for God to work in your life, and in the lives of those who have wronged you. As you forgive, you will reign in life as a king over circumstances, disappointments, and sorrow.

Forgiveness produces:

> peace,
>
> reconciliation,
>
> harmony,
>
> understanding,
>
> fellowship.

Unforgiveness produces:

> strife,
>
> bitterness,
>
> disharmony,
>
> hatred,
>
> war.

At times, the whole human race is in danger of being overwhelmed by these evil, negative forces. We, as Christians, are to shine as lights in a dark world. We are to be a forgiving people!

> And when ye stand praying, forgive, if ye have
> aught against any: that your Father also which
> is in heaven may forgive you your trespasses.
>
> Mark 11:25

Ought means anything and everything, big or small, even
almost nothing at all. *Any* means everybody. We are to
forgive everybody for anything and everything they have
done to hurt us.

Obviously, the most hurtful areas of our lives need to be
forgiven. Jesus said the most minute detail must be
forgiven, also.

Sometimes we need to forgive a person who is dead. Unforgiveness is equally as harmful in our lives whether the
person is living or dead.

Many times the hardest person to forgive is oneself. We
make many mistakes, yet we have to learn to accept those
mistakes as being a part of our past. We have to press
on. Jesus taught us to forgive if we have ought against
anyone, and that includes ourselves.

People want to receive from God, but they do not want
to talk about unforgiveness. "I want to be healed of cancer,
but I do not want to talk about unforgiveness!", they say.
"I want to be healed of ulcers, but I do not want to talk
about unforgiveness!" Unforgiveness is often the root of
the problem.

When Jesus was in Bethany, He passed a fig tree.

> And seeing a fig tree afar off having leaves, he
> came, if haply he might find any thing thereon:
> and when he came to it, he found nothing but
> leaves; for the time of figs was not yet.
>
> And Jesus answered and said unto it, No man
> eat fruit of thee hereafter for ever. And his
> disciples heard it.
>
> Mark 11:13-14

There were two areas of that fig tree—the SEEN and the UNSEEN. There was a part that you could see and a part you could not see. The part that could not be seen was the root system.

We have a root system. Our root system is the unseen part of us—the spirit person.

When Jesus spoke to that fig tree, His words took effect in the unseen area. It later manifested in the seen area. Jesus knew that the unseen area was where the tree received its life. The Word of the Lord took effect immediately in the unseen area, or root system.

If we want results in the seen area—our physical bodies—we must learn to care for the root system properly.

The Bible teaches us that bitterness has a root.

> Follow peace with all men, and holiness, without
> which no man shall see the Lord:
>
> Looking diligently lest any man fail of the grace

> of God; lest any root of bitterness springing up
> trouble you, and thereby many be defiled.
>
> Hebrews 12:14-15

You may say, "Brother Osteen, I do not have the power
to forgive. I was so mistreated as a child." Yes, you do.
You can forgive because God provided forgiveness at the
Cross for you. You are forgiven, not because you deserve
it, but by grace.

By the grace provided at the Cross, you have the power
necessary to forgive others.

> Surely he hath borne our griefs, and carried our
> sorrows: yet we did esteem him stricken, smit-
> ten of God, and afflicted.
>
> But he was wounded for our transgressions, he
> was bruised for our iniquities: the chastisement
> of our peace was upon him; and with his stripes
> we are healed.
>
> All we like sheep have gone astray; we have
> turned every one to his own way; and the Lord
> hath laid on him the iniquity of us all.
>
> Isaiah 53:4-6

Only on the basis of the atoning death of Jesus Christ on
the Cross can we receive forgiveness from God.

Only on the basis of the grace of God offered to us by His
death can we offer forgiveness to others.

> But God forbid that I should glory, save in the

cross of our Lord Jesus Christ, by whom the
world is crucified unto me, and I unto the world.

Galatians 6:14

It was at the Cross that Jesus cancelled every claim of
Satan on our lives.

Forgiveness is a DECISION. You must choose to forgive
whether you feel like it or not. As you stand on that decision, God in you will love the person who has wronged you.
One day, you will suddenly realize that you cannot even
remember the wrong they committed against you.

Receiving the forgiveness of God is also a DECISION. You
choose to believe that God's Word is true. If God said He
would forgive you, then He will. You may not deserve it,
but forgiveness is yours because He loves you and desires
fellowship with you. There is no condemnation to those
who are in Christ Jesus. (Romans 8:1)

David prayed a beautiful prayer for the forgiveness of his
sins. He desired to be set apart to God.

> Have mercy upon me, O God, according to thy
> lovingkindness: according unto the multitude
> of thy tender mercies blot out my trans-
> gressions.
>
> Wash me throughly from mine iniquity, and
> cleanse me from my sin.
>
> For I acknowledge my transgressions: and my
> sin is ever before me.

Behold, thou desirest truth in the inward parts: and in the hidden part thou shalt make me to know wisdom.

Purge me with hyssop, and I shall be clean: wash me, and I shall be whiter than snow.

Make me to hear joy and gladness; that the bones which thou hast broken may rejoice.

Hide thy face from my sins, and blot out all mine iniquities.

Create in me a clean heart, O God; and renew a right spirit within me.

Cast me not away from thy presence; and take not thy holy spirit from me.

Restore unto me the joy of thy salvation; and uphold me with thy free spirit.

Then will I teach transgressors thy ways; and sinners shall be converted unto thee.

Psalm 51:1-3, 6-13

We can pray the same prayer that David prayed. The Bible says that David was a man after God's own heart.

Praise God, we have been forgiven, and we have the power to forgive others through Jesus Christ!

WE REIGN IN LIFE AS KINGS
THROUGH FORGIVENESS.

Eight

Reigning in Life Through the Power of Humility

Humility is the secret to continual usefulness in the kingdom of God. We can truly reign in life as kings through the power of humility.

> By humility and the fear of the Lord are riches,
> and honour, and life.
>
> Proverbs 22:4

God greatly rewards the man or woman who lives a life of humility.

Humility is not weakness. It is a total lack of confidence in your own ability, and a total dependence on God's ability.

All Christians should learn to walk in the spirit of humility. It is a very important attitude, and the Word of God has much to say about it.

> I therefore, the prisoner for the Lord, appeal

to and beg you to walk (lead a life) worthy of
the [divine] calling to which you have been
called—with behavior that is a credit to the
summons to God's service,

Living as becomes you—with complete
lowliness of mind (humility) and meekness
(unselfishness, gentleness, mildness), with patience, bearing with one another and making
allowances because you love one another.

                                        Ephesians 4:1-2
                                        (Amplified)

Many people are used by God for a short period of time,
but humility is the key to continual usefulness.

For by the grace (unmerited favor of God) given
to me I warn every one among you not to
estimate and think of himself more highly than
he ought—not to have an exaggerated opinion
of his own importance; but to rate his ability
with sober judgment, each according to the
degree of faith apportioned by God to him.

                                        Romans 12:3
                                        (Amplified)

This passage of scripture is a warning to believers. We
must realize that all blessings come from God. All that
we are, and all that we have is a result of the grace of God
in our lives.

I am continually aware of the fact that the good that is
done in Lakewood Church is a result of the work of the
Holy Spirit. God saved me at the age of seventeen when
I was selling popcorn in a theater. It is only by the grace
of God that I am able to minister to others.

Pride and an exaggerated opinion of yourself will cut off your usefulness. You may think, "Well, they do not have the respect for me that they ought to have! After all, I'm somebody!" That is an exaggerated opinion of your importance.

I realize that the only authority that I have as a Pastor is a spiritual, intangible authority that Jesus gives me. If He withdraws that authority, I have absolutely nothing.

God sets many ministries in the Church. We should always hold one another in high esteem because God has a special work for each of us. Every ministry is important.

> For as we have many members in one body, and all members have not the same office:
>
> So we, being many, are one body in Christ, and every one members one of another.
>
> Having then gifts differing according to the grace that is given to us, whether prophecy, let us prophesy according to the proportion of faith;
>
> Or ministry, let us wait on our ministering: or he that teacheth, on teaching;
>
> Or he that exhorteth, on exhortation: he that giveth, let him do it with simplicity; he that ruleth, with diligence; he that sheweth mercy, with cheerfulness.
>
> Romans 12:4-8

Our responsibility is to function in the ministry that God has given us. Not every person is called into one of the five-fold ministries. God is using lay people all over the world in supernatural ways. Every ministry is necessary for the perfecting and full equipping of the saints.

We need to give unqualified courtesy to every person. We should never treat anyone disrespectfully, especially a child of God.

> But he giveth more grace. Wherefore he saith, God resisteth the proud, but giveth grace unto the humble.
>
> James 4:6

Pride destroys the flow of God in our lives. God resists the proud. He does not just resist proud laymen, He resists proud preachers. He resists proud wives. God resists the proud and gives grace to the humble.

We all need the grace of God in our lives!

The Apostle Paul had a beautiful spirit of humility. He said, "I can do all things THROUGH CHRIST which strengtheneth me." (Philippians 4:13) Again Paul confessed, "I am more than a conqueror THROUGH HIM that loved me."(Romans 8:37) Paul spoke of the mighty works that he could do through Jesus. Our confession should be what we have in Christ, and not what we can do in our own power and ability.

In his silent, sober moments, Paul, remembering what a mess he had made of his life before he knew Jesus, said,

"I am the least of the apostles." (I Corinthians 15:9) Paul was a man who knew within himself that he was not worthy of the least of the mercies of God, yet he knew who he was in Jesus. That is a man who can shake nations!

> Not that we are sufficient of ourselves to think any thing as of ourselves; but our sufficiency is of God.
>
> II Corinthians 3:5

What good thing do we have that we have not received from God? He is our sufficiency. He is our source of life.

Humility is the key to continual usefulness in the kingdom of God.

Let's study the life of Moses.

> Now the man Moses was very meek, above all the men which were upon the face of the earth.
>
> Numbers 12:3

Moses was the most humble man on the face of the earth, and God used him in a mighty way. Many people think Moses was ignorant because of his humility, but Stephen spoke very highly of him, by inspiration of the Holy Spirit.

> And Moses was learned in all the wisdom of the Egyptians, and was mighty in words and in deeds.
>
> Acts 7:22

Egypt was the greatest and most advanced nation of Moses' day. Moses had all the privileges of its universities.

He was a mighty orator, and the Bible says that he was mighty in deeds.

God revealed to Moses that he would be the deliverer of the children of Israel, but he was not yet ready. In all his pride, Moses slew an Egyptian who was fighting with a fellow Hebrew. He thought the children of Israel would understand that he was chosen to be their deliverer. (Acts 7:23-25)

Moses felt he was well able to deliver the Israelites from their bondage in Egypt. He had the ability to speak and do great works. He was ready to do the job. He probably even felt that God had chosen him because of his great ability!

Moses was a proud man. He felt he was sufficient, but he was not. He had the call of God upon his life, but he was not ready for God to trust him with that task.

Forty years later, on the back side of the desert, Moses had still not fulfilled the call of God. He felt defeated, but God appeared to him in a burning bush and spoke to him.

> Come now therefore, and I will send thee unto Pharaoh, that thou mayest bring forth my people the children of Israel out of Egypt.
>
> And Moses said unto God, Who am I, that I should go unto Pharaoh, and that I should bring forth the children of Israel out of Egypt?
>
> Exodus 3:10-11

The first words that Moses spoke were, "Who am I?" Forty years before he thought, "Here I am! I am God's great deliverer!" Here is a man who had all the skills and learning of the Egyptians. The Bible says that he was mighty in word, yet Moses argues, "I am not eloquent. I am slow of speech and tongue." (Exodus 4:10) Was Moses lying? No! He finally realized that without God he was nothing. Only by the power of God could he bring deliverance to the children of Israel.

> And Moses answered and said, But, behold, they will not believe me, nor hearken unto my voice: for they will say, The Lord hath not appeared unto thee.
>
> And the Lord said unto him, What is that in thine hand? And he said, A rod.
>
> And he said, Cast it on the ground. And he cast it on the ground, and it became a serpent; and Moses fled from before it.
>
> And the Lord said unto Moses, Put forth thine hand, and take it by the tail. And he put forth his hand, and caught it, and it became a rod in his hand:
>
> That they may believe that the Lord God of their fathers, the God of Abraham, the God of Isaac, and the God of Jacob, hath appeared unto thee.
>
> Exodus 4:1-5

God showed Moses that he could depend on the power of God. Moses marched out of Egypt with three million slaves, waving the rod of God in his hand. This time, God

was with him. Moses learned to reign in life through the
spirit of humility.

God uses and exalts many men and women. Unfortunately,
some believers get a touch of the blessing of God, and then
become proud and haughty. That is a dangerous place to
be.

Oral Roberts once said, "The most dangerous time in a
man's life is when he feels so sufficient that he does not
need faith in God."

The most dangerous place is that secure place where you
think you have it made. You have all the money you need.
You have no challenges. You have no need to trust God
and His power.

I encourage you to forever extend yourself to the place
where God must work for you.

Moses chose to humble himself, and God blessed him
mightily, but soon criticism came from the mouths of his
own brother and sister.

> And Miriam and Aaron spake against Moses
> because of the Ethiopian woman whom he had
> married: for he had married an Ethiopian
> woman.
>
> And they said, Hath the Lord indeed spoken on-
> ly by Moses? hath he not spoken also by us?
> And the Lord heard it.
>
> Numbers 12:1-2

Miriam and Aaron became critical of Moses. Miriam had taken care of Moses when he was a child. The Bible says that she was a prophetess. Aaron was the spokesman for the children of Israel. Their critical attitudes caused them to have an exaggerated opinion of their importance. They thought, "Is Moses the only one who can talk to God? After all, God has spoken to us, too!"

I have had a few people take that attitude in our church. My responsibility is to keep order in the services. I try to operate in love, and to protect the congregation. I have had people stand up in the middle of a service and give a revelation that is totally out of order. When I asked them to sit down and wait, they got mad and stormed out, saying, "Bless God, is he the only one who knows how to move in the Spirit?" That is an ugly attitude, and it is not scriptural.

You will never grow in the Lord if you do not respect the leadership God sets over a congregation. Any revelation can be held in your spirit until the right time to give it. I have held a prophecy in my spirit for a day or two. You may think, "God gave it to me and I cannot control it." If you cannot control it, it is not of God.

The Bible says that when Miriam and Aaron spoke against Moses, God heard it. We never have a right to criticize anyone. Every child of God has an important function in the Body of Christ. God sees His children differently than we see them. Notice what He said about Moses:

> My servant Moses is not so, who is faithful in all mine house.

> With him will I speak mouth to mouth, even ap-
> parently, and not in dark speeches; and the
> similitude of the Lord shall he behold: wherefore
> then were ye not afraid to speak against my ser-
> vant Moses?
>
> Numbers 12:7-8

God had spoken to Moses face to face, and yet they were
critical of him. Miriam and Aaron had been chosen for a
great task. Why should they be jealous of Moses? They
should have been glad for the ministry that God had given
them.

Miriam and Aaron's critical and proud attitude provoked the anger of God, and Miriam was struck with
leprosy. Moses interceded on her behalf and God healed
her, but the Iraelites' journey was delayed for seven days.
The whole move of God was stopped because two people
had exaggerated opinions of their importance.

Miriam and Aaron's attitude cut off their usefulness, until they repented. When God begins to use you in the gifts
of the Holy Spirit, when He begins to bless you and give
you revelations, let it humble you more and more. It is
not you, it is God.

Let's examine the life of King Saul in the Old Testament.
Saul was a fine-looking man. The Bible says that he was
head and shoulders above all the rest of the men. (I Samuel
9:2) He was the first king over Israel, and God used him
mightily. However, Saul disobeyed God and fell from favor
with Him. The Prophet Samuel interceded on Saul's behalf,
but God rejected Saul as king. God spoke through

Samuel and made a statement about Saul's attitude that
we should always remember.

> And Samuel said, When thou wast little in thine
> own sight, wast thou not made the head of the
> tribes of Israel, and the Lord anointed thee king
> over Israel?
>
> 1 Samuel 15:17

"When thou wast little in thine own sight . . ." That is the
secret. When we are little in our own eyes, God is pleased
with us because we know that we can do nothing without
Him. If we will have a low estimation of our own importance, God will use us.

> Pride goeth before destruction, and an haughty
> spirit before a fall.
>
> Proverbs 16:18

> Before destruction the heart of man is haughty,
> and before honour is humility.
>
> Proverbs 18:12

Let your confession be what you have in Christ, and not
what you can do in your own power and ability.

Many great men of God have spent years doing the insignificant tasks that God asked them to do. The Bible
encourages us not to despise the day of small beginnings.
(Zechariah 4:10)

> He that is faithful in that which is least is
> faithful also in much: and he that is unjust in
> the least is unjust also in much.
>
> Luke 16:10

When you prove faithful to God in the little things, then He will trust you with much.

In the Book of Acts, the number of disciples increased and there arose a problem with serving tables and distributing clothing and food. The twelve disciples felt that they should give themselves continually to prayer and the preaching of the Word of God, therefore, they appointed seven men to handle the food and clothing.

> Then the twelve called the multitude of the disciples unto them, and said, It is not reason that we should leave the word of God, and serve tables.
>
> Wherefore, brethren, look ye out among you seven men of honest report, full of the Holy Ghost and wisdom, whom we may appoint over this business.
>
> Acts 6:2-3

These seven men were not just ordinary men. The Bible says they were full of the Holy Ghost and wisdom. They were powerful men, and yet they were chosen to serve tables and distribute clothing.

These men could have said, "I am not called to serve tables. God called me to preach." They could have had an exaggerated opinion of their importance, but they were faithful to do what needed to be done.

> Humble yourselves therefore under the mighty hand of God, that he may exalt you in due time.
>
> I Peter 5:6

God will bless people who are willing to take a lower position in the eyes of men. He will exalt the humble.

It was not long until Stephen began to shine. He was one of those who was faithful to serve tables. Stephen became a powerful preacher. He did great wonders and miracles among the people. The Bible says that no one was able to resist the wisdom and the Spirit by which he spoke. (Acts 6:8-10) Soon Stephen was arrested and taken to the council, but everyone who looked at him saw that his face was shining like the face of an angel.

The power of God in Stephen's life provoked the anger of his enemies, and they dragged him out of the city and stoned him to death. The heavens were opened and Stephen saw the glory of God.

> But he, being full of the Holy Ghost, looked up stedfastly into heaven, and saw the glory of God, and Jesus standing on the right hand of God,
>
> And said, Behold, I see the heavens opened, and the Son of man standing on the right hand of God.
>
> Acts 7:55-56

Stephen said, "I see Jesus STANDING on the right hand of God." Jesus is SEATED at the right hand of the Father. I believe that Jesus thought, "In honor to Stephen, I will stand to receive his spirit. I will stand for a man who was faithful to serve tables. I will stand for a man who will give his life for the sake of the Gospel."

God honors men and women who will do humble tasks for Him.

Philip was another disciple who waited on tables. He began to preach in Samaria and the whole city was stirred by miracles, signs, and wonders. (Acts 8:6-8)

An angel of God appeared to Philip and sent him to the desert to lead an Ethiopian man to the Lord. After baptizing this man, Philip was supernaturally translated to the city of Azotus, where he began preaching.

That is what happens to the person who will walk humbly before the Lord. The man who lives a life of humility is the man who will walk in the supernatural power of God.

Let there be no fighting over the high positions. Give unqualified courtesy and respect to every person. Serve one another in love. Walk humbly before God, and you will be blessed with riches, honor, and life.

WE REIGN IN LIFE AS KINGS
THROUGH THE POWER OF HUMILITY.

WE REIGN IN LIFE AS KINGS BY ONE,
CHRIST JESUS.